HELL'S BEGINNING

By

John T. M. Herres

A HellBound Books LLC
Publication

www.hellboundbookspublishing.com

Printed in the United States of America

Dedicated to my Son, Terry M. Herres

With Special Thanks to:

Ryan Harker, for attempting to assist me in the writing of this story.
Some of his ideas are still present.

Mary F. Davis
Thomas I. Herres
Lynda L. Herres
Thomas L. Herres
Judith (Judy) Ann Colella
http://https://www.facebook.com/judith.colella?fref=ts
Anthony Vidal--
https://www.facebook.com/anthonyvidal
Toneye Eyenot--
https://www.facebook.com/toneyeblakk
Sandy Fosdick
https://www.facebook.com/sandy.fosdick.3
Roma Gray
https://www.facebook.com/romagray

And Many Others for their support and encouragement.

John T. M. Herres

HELL'S BEGINNING

Hell's Beginning

Captive

There she lay, in all her splendor. Naked as the day she was born, but with more endowments than any one person should be allowed. Her overly large breasts sagged to both sides and made her half-dollar-sized brown areolas seem to be mounted under her armpits. They jiggled back and forth with her erratic breathing like runny, half-cooked eggs.

With her arms pulled up above her head and tied to the stakes I had driven into the ground for just this purpose, and her beefy legs pulled apart by her ankles tied in the same fashion, she resembled a naked swimmer frozen in the middle of a synchronized event. But she wasn't frozen, she was very animated, or at least as much as the bindings would allow.

The red bandana rolled up and tied around her face to produce a gag pulled her mouth drastically wide, as I had forced it far behind her front teeth, causing her tongue to either be secured to her bottom jaw or pushed almost down her throat. Whichever, it made no difference to me, as long as it muffled her incessant pleas to be released, that she wouldn't tell anyone.

Yea, how many times had that offer ever really

worked? Like I would suddenly realize that I made a mistake, cut her bonds, and apologize profusely; maybe even take her to dinner trying to make it up to her, and strike a bargain for neither of us to mention or think about it again.

No, I had my mind made up, her fate now sealed. It had been ever since she made the error of approaching me at the bar earlier that night.

I hadn't gone there looking for this, just stopped in for a beer before acquiring a motel room for the night in anticipation of resuming my journey the next day. In search of I don't know what.

I procured my drink and commandeered a small table in the back corner of the room. I sat with my back against the wall to watch the frivolity of the locals as they went through their weekly, if not daily ritual of unwinding after a hard day's activities.

Being a Friday night, the bar could have been more packed than usual, with those who had just gotten paid popping in to celebrate another week down the drain. Most probably had hopes of finding some new company to go home with.

From my hiding spot, I spied a goddess sitting with her girlfriend at the bar. She looked perfect, dressed in a modest, mid-thigh length, baby blue dress. She had pulled her long, wavy, satin-looking black hair back into a ponytail reaching the middle of her back. I could imagine its softness were I allowed to run my fingers through it.

As far as I could tell, she wore little to no makeup, yet I had never seen a more beautiful little pixie-like being. With her slight stature, she almost had to climb onto the stool to reach over the top of the bar.

I also noticed how young she looked, as did the bartender, obviously, for he looked at her ID before serving her. Or maybe he just wanted an easy way to find out her name, or perhaps where she lived. Who knew?

My view was abruptly blocked. I casually looked up to see this side of beef looming before me. Though not repulsive, either in the face or her physique, neither were to my liking. Most people would consider her big boned. To me, she carried some 20 pounds extra weight and needed a severe breast reduction.

She wore a loose, red silk blouse tucked in at the waist and unbuttoned almost to her bra, allowing her more than ample melons to show a cleavage that could almost hide a full-sized flashlight. Her black mini skirt looked at least two sizes too small. I guessed she must have spent close to 15 minutes rolling and scooting across the floor, hunching her hips towards the ceiling trying to pull it up, then to fasten it around herself. Even in the dim light this far away from the others, I could tell the seams were stretched to their limit. I silently praised the manufacturer for such sturdy stitching.

On her feet were a pair of stilettos any self-respecting (or self-loathing?) hooker would kill for. Glittery-gold and all of five inches high. I was surprised she could stand straight, let alone walk given her top-heavy condition. She did waver slightly, which I concluded had something to do with the rum and cola drink, now almost empty, and figured it had not been her first of the evening.

In a terrible slur, which I'm sure sounded to her like a sultry voice, she greeted me with, "Hi, Handsome! Buy me a drink?" With the drunken tongue mixed with poor learning and a deep, country accent, I actually heard, "Ha, Hansm! Bah meuh drnk?"

As I finally glanced up at her face, I saw she had deep, red lipstick on her almost pouting lips, and too much rouge on her cheeks, mixed with inebriation, making her look almost comical. Her light brown eyes were near half closed, the lids plastered with too much two-toned blue shadow and her lashes smeared with gobs of mascara. Her eyeliner extended out past the actual edge of her eyes, looking more like a Cleopatra wannabe than a modern woman on the make. Her wiry brown hair had been pulled back into a loose ponytail and a couple of strands had worked out and hung unevenly at her temples.

"Sorry, but I'm about to leave," I responded, deciding to avoid making a scene and find my way out. I really didn't want to hurt her feelings by saying that she was just too large for my tastes.

I scooted back in the chair and glanced again at the dream at the bar. 'Big Boobs' followed my gaze. Seeing the girl, she remarked, "Huh, is *that* what you want? A little girl? Can't handle a ***real*** woman, huh?"

I narrowed my eyes at her, my brow furrowing as I stood up. Her eyes grew wider as I achieved all of my 6-and-a-half-foot height. I had on a pair of blue jeans, not tight but wore a belt to secure them at my waist. A matching denim shirt with faux tiger's eye buttons up the front.

She appraised me, looking me up and down as I had done her. At 230 pounds, mostly muscle with the tell-tale minor flab at my hips trying to advertise my age, I must say I still cut an impressive image.

I ran my fingers through my slightly disheveled blond hair, which could have used a trim, and glared at her with my jet-black eyes. I saw a shiver run through her as she pressed her thighs together involuntarily.

I leaned towards her upturned face, smothered with so many cosmetics, and told her if I happened to see a "real" (making quotes in the air with my fingers) woman, I'd be able to handle her just fine.

Not even finishing the rest of my drink, I walked away, intending for that to be the last time I had any interaction with her. She had other ideas, and almost bellowed to my back, "I bet you couldn't even get it up for a real woman, only little girls!" Then she laughed derisively.

I clenched both my jaw and my left fist. With extreme effort I continued out the door, knowing that several sets of eyes were glancing back and forth from her to my back.

Getting into my fully restored, 40-year-old classic station wagon, I began breathing deeply in and out, my eyes closed, calming my anger and my heartbeat, relaxing the death grip I had on my steering wheel. I felt as if time had slowed to a crawl as my mind's eye saw the ideal solution to this situation. I had no intention of just letting it slide and once again stuffing the feelings down inside of me.

Starting the engine, I drove a couple of blocks to the motel and paid the clerk for two days, with the explicit instructions not to be disturbed, not even for maid service. I unloaded some of my belongings and went back to the bar to wait for her.

After closing time, I finally saw her exit all alone. I tilted my head forward, keeping my eyes on her as she stumbled toward the only vehicle left on the customer's side of the lot, a beat up, mid-'80's, blue pickup. I felt an evil grin tug the corners of my mouth.

She stopped beside her truck and looked around. I don't know if she didn't see my car or just figured it to be empty because all my windows were limo-tinted. She lifted her skirt, lowered her panties, and hunkered down to piss into the dirt right out in the open, dark lot.

I sensed my time to move. I got out of my vehicle and noiselessly trotted to where she relieved herself. She bent her head down as her stream trickled to a stop. Before she could right herself, I balled up my fist and hit her as hard as I could on the left side of her face causing her head to bounce off the side of her truck. She hadn't even seen me. I could have left then, but I had a definite plan of action.

After moving my car over beside her spot, I opened the tailgate, picked her up and unceremoniously tossed her in, her red, lacy, thong-style panties still around her knees. I pulled them the rest of the way off, then the remainder of her clothes, and tossed them all in the back of her truck next to her purse, which she had slung there before taking care of her business. For general knowledge, I used my knuckle to pry the wallet open and get her name. "Sharon Burlowski." What a name.

As I drove away, I made sure to kick up the dirt with my tires. I headed away from town, remembering a broken down old farm I had passed earlier that day on my way in. At the rustic gate, I put on some thick leather gloves before getting out. The rusty nail in the dry rotted pole which held the locked chain in place came free with ease. After moving the car through, I closed the gate and firmly forced the nail back into the same hole.

I heard her moan, so opened the tailgate and pulled her to a sitting position. I watched her eyes began fluttering as she reached a hand up to the sore spot on the left side of her face and uttered another moan. Her eyelids flapped when she opened them. Looking downward, she realized she was without clothing and saw my boots.

As her gaze traveled up, I balled my fist again and raised it beside my head. When she saw my face, then my raised fist, she began to try to lift both of her hands in defense. I pushed her hands down and swung straight at her as she turned slightly to her left and started to say, "No!"

I connected solidly, my knuckles covering her whole right cheek as she was knocked back into my car and out cold at the same time. I shoved her legs back in and closed the tailgate, then proceeded down the driveway to find a usable building on the derelict property.

After following several turns, I rounded a curve and saw the opportune spot. A dilapidated building just across from the main house. It looked to have been either the maid's quarters or a "mother-in-law" house but appeared mostly stable. Reaching into my glove box, I took out my flashlight and left the car to explore the building and grounds around it.

Upon entering, I saw some decaying furniture, probably left behind when the property had been abandoned, all sitting on an earthen floor. Multiple cockroaches and a few mice scurried away because of my trespassing.

Around back, I found stacks of decaying lumber, most rotted away. I also found some old metal T-posts, rusted through in some spots, but enough left solid to suit my purposes, as well as a partially unraveled roll of leftover fence wire.

Still wearing the gloves, I picked up eight posts, no less than 3ft long each, and the wire and took them inside the shanty.

I went back out to my car and pulled Sharon out, slung her over my shoulder and carried her in. I laid her flat on her back and positioned her as I wanted, then began driving the posts into the packed dirt with the hammer I kept with my assorted tools. I used plenty of the wire to secure each ankle and wrist to a stake.

With that chore completed, I pulled the remains of the couch closer to await her awakening, then stood the flashlight on end to illuminate as much of the room as possible and lit a cigarette.

Before long, she began squirming. I sparked another cig and stood so she could see just who had done this to her. As she regained consciousness, she started to pull alternately at her arms and legs trying to rise. She realized quickly she was trapped, and when she saw me again, began to cry and utter apologies and pleas for me not to hurt her, to which I had to laugh.

"You mean I haven't hurt you yet?"

"Yes, you have!" she wailed, "But it's OK... If you let me go, I'll pretend nothing happened! I won't tell anyone! I promise!" Her swollen face and erratic breathing caused her words to slur, much like the alcohol had earlier.

"And what will you say of the bruises on your face, wrists, and ankles?"

"I'll just say I fell; anyone who saw me last night would believe that!"

We bantered on, her thinking up lies she promised to tell whenever I posed a problem. I enjoyed the game: She thought her tears, cries, and pleas would make an impression on me, while I knew I would be the only one to leave that abandoned farm.

"I have money!" she declared, her eyes opening as far as the swelling would allow.

"Oh yeah?" Her declaration intrigued me. "What money? How could someone like you have any money?"

She averted her eyes, not wanting to give the answer. When she looked back, she said, "In my truck, in the glove box. There's three envelopes, each has about $50,000 in it." Unknowingly, she had just given all of them to me.

"We'll see, but we're gonna have a little fun first," I lied. With a chuckle, I continued, "I am, anyway."

I pivoted and headed toward the door. I had finished playing and had a few more preparations before getting to the end of the game. She began wailing and crying again as my gloved hand closed around the knob.

She yelled, "No! Wait! You can't just leave me here!"

Turning to her, I used a sinister near-whisper which caused her eyes to go wider. "You're mistaken. I am the one of us who *can* leave here."

She began her screaming anew before I even made it back to my car. More out of exasperation of her trilling voice than from fear of someone hearing her, I went into my tool stash and retrieved a dirty old bandana. Re-entering, I began rolling it up. I knelt beside her and violently shoved it between her teeth, telling her she was grating my nerves with her annoying voice. I tied it behind her head, intentionally catching some of her hair in the knot.

I decided to drive back to the motel to get some sleep before I continued with my plans. It had been a very long day, indeed, and I would need to be fresh for the next steps.

On the way, I passed by the bar and saw two furtive forms reaching into the back of her truck. I knew they were rifling through her belongings and smiled. Their fingerprints would be all over the place. How fortuitous!

Sharon Burlowski

Sharon felt used up. She believed she had always been lied to: By her parents, by her so-called friends, and most especially by men.

All her life, she had been told she could do anything with herself, but since she never believed it, she never had. She sensed her worthlessness, that she would never amount to anything, and her whole life had been one long evolution toward that state of being.

She had finally made it there, she had hit rock bottom. Like any other cornered beast, she was desperate and would do anything to get out of her situation, and just like every other insecure low-life out there, it was all about trying to save number one.

On the surface, she would never admit that her life was anything less than exactly how she wanted it to be. However, her intentions always ended up being derailed by cheap booze and sex; nothing seemed to go right for the delinquent, train-wrecked woman. The hooch was why she could, for the most part anyway, stay safe in her delusion that she had a purpose. In reality, she was nothing more than a middle-aged, overweight divorcee who had been working at the Charity Falls Savings & Loan for the last six years in the same position.

Charity Falls, Utah. An almost picturesque small town ideal. The business-lined Main Street most always had cars parked on the curbs; the people walked around offering fake smiles and greetings to neighbors and strangers alike; the hypocrisy so thick it could make one gag. She hated everything there, almost as much as she hated herself, but couldn't afford to leave.

So, Sharon had started what she liked to call a "savings plan." Though she would tell no one about it, she meant to someday use it to leave the sweet little township for greener pastures. She knew if she could just break free of the towns' stranglehold on her life she could actually be somebody; maybe then her life could finally have real meaning.

She wouldn't ever tell anyone about her savings plan because it involved quite a bit of illegality. For the last 18 months, she had been embezzling money from her job at the Savings & Loan. Not a whole lot when she started, but the numbers quickly began adding up and then the temptation to take a little more became too much for her to resist. She quietly skimmed a small amount from every deposit she handled for the bank's customers.

They would hand her the money, she would count it out and make the receipt, even enter it into the computer with the correct numbers. But as the green went into the drawer, one bill would go into her pocket. Sometimes it would only be a ten or twenty-dollar bill, but occasionally a larger bill would "fall" out of the stack.

At home, she stashed it all in old coffee cans and hid them wherever she could around her mobile home. She waited until she thought there might be enough to leave. Hopefully, she could be on the west coast for Christmas.

Sharon cursed loudly as she banged her shin on the low coffee table that sat in front of her matching, tattered, faded green couch and loveseat. As she stumbled on, favoring the offended appendage, she put thoughts of her wicked schemes on the back burner and concentrated on that night. Being Friday night, she wanted two things; to get drunk and find some action with a man.

She stumble-hopped her way down the narrow hall of her dilapidated singlewide trailer to the bathroom and ran a warm bubble bath. While she waited for the tub to fill she headed back to the kitchen to refresh her favorite drink to enjoy while she soaked; rum and cola. Drink in hand, she headed back to the tub and was just in time to stop the water before suds overflowed onto the floor.

Sharon set her drink amidst the clutter under the mirror and, gazing at her reflection, stared into her own brown eyes.

Pulling off her oversized tee shirt she examined herself in the mirror. As she admired her large breasts, she thought, "What man wouldn't want to play with these babies?" She smirked and looked at the bulge of her belly. Rubbing a hand down herself, she tested her firmness by grabbing a handful of her flesh and jiggling it. She sighed again, knowing she was not as fit as she used to be, yet realizing she would always be too lazy to do anything about it.

She took a couple of gulps of her drink and then turned to the bath and stepped carefully in. Lowering herself gingerly into the hot water, she felt delicious shivers course through her entire body and sighed gently. The nearly full tub threatened to overflow onto the tiled floor. She didn't waste much time before scrubbing her body to feel more refreshed for the evenings' activities.

After climbing out, she wrapped her hair in one towel and began scrubbing herself dry with another. She drained her drink and the tub

She pulled out her favorite blouse, the red, silky one, and fished through her skirts for something to match. When she came upon the little black number, she remembered she hadn't worn it in some time. It was perfect. No man in his right mind would be able to resist her in that ensemble. She went to her dresser and pulled out her red, lacy bra and the matching "t-back" panties to complete the set and began to dress.

As she pulled the skirt over her thighs, she got some resistance. She knew it would fit, it just had to. Sliding her fingers from front to back, hitching side to side and thrusting her hips forward repetitively, she only managed to move it little bits at a time.

Finally, she had it up, but when she went to fasten the clasp, she found it shy by a quarter inch. She sucked air in and blew it out, then inhaled deeply and yanked the fabric side to side trying to get it fastened. Finally, the clasp caught, and she quickly pulled up the zipper before she relaxed. "As long as it holds, it doesn't matter how I got it there," she mumbled to herself.

She went about pulling out the coffee cans she had stashed throughout her trailer. She found that the thin walls of the mobile home were quite easy to patch over, so had made several places where she could put the small plastic containers as she filled them.

Moving pictures and some small furniture, she collected all the canisters from their hidey-holes, placing them on her kitchen table. She emptied them and began smoothing the bills out, stacking them according to their face value. Then she began counting.

When she had finished her chore, she couldn't believe her tally. One hundred eighty-three thousand, eight hundred two dollars. She counted again, unable to accept that she had been so successful. Sure enough, her count came out the same.

"Oh, muh gahd," she exclaimed to the empty house. "$183,802.00. Holy shit! I think I've got enough to bail now."

She began figuring in her head all the things she could do with that kind of money. By her standards, she was now rich. She would be able to start fresh somewhere else, someplace that had never heard of Charity Falls, Utah. Maybe Southern California, where it stayed sunny all year round, never got cold. She could lie on the beach all day, soak up the rays and flirt with all the cute guys, sipping on margaritas with those little paper umbrellas on top.

Better yet, she should go to Mexico, where a hundred thousand bucks would be a veritable fortune. She could live the rest of her life in luxury in good old "May-hee-coe!"

She gathered the bills up and divided them into equal piles. Then she got out three envelopes and put all but three hundred two dollars in them. By her calculations, that would be almost $50,000.00 in each envelope, and plenty enough in her pocket to party down that night. She could call it her "going away" party.

In the morning, she wouldn't even worry about packing a lot of stuff. She would climb in her truck and just drive away, never to step foot in this crummy little town again. Somewhere in Arizona, she would get rid of the truck and get a nice little car. With air conditioning. Then she'd find a way across the border and head as far into Central America as she could get.

She put one envelope in her purse, just in case she needed it, and decided she could stash the other two in the glove box. They should be alright there as long as she locked it while at the bar.

She was ready to party. The excitement of finding out just how well her plan had worked had left her parched and her heart still beat wildly in her chest. She went into the bathroom and splashed herself with her favorite cologne, 'Lady Stetson'.

After locking her front door, she climbed into her old blue Ford and headed to Pop Inn, the local watering hole. She frequently showed up there and knew on Friday nights there would always be someone with whom she could share a little private time. Many times, she went into the men's room and either performed fellatio or had a quickie. That night, however, she wanted to find someone to take her home. To a real bed.

She walked in and saw many familiar faces. Stopping at the bar, she ordered a rum and cola, then changed her mind. "Make that a margarita, Jack!"

"Hey! Celebrating something, Sharon?" The bartender had been serving her for many years, and never saw her drink anything other than rum and cola. He figured something was up, but it was his job to make what the people ordered, so he began the preparations.

"Yea," Sharon hollered back, "you could call it my retirement party!" She walked away, leaving Jack with a confused look as he finished her frozen concoction.

Sharon wiggled her way to the dance floor as the jukebox blared a country line-dance song, and she took a place in the line of people already there. The waitress caught her eye as she placed her order on a table, so Sharon made her way to it after the song was finished.

Her drink, though cold and refreshing, did not fuel the buzz she planned on obtaining, so when she finished it, she ordered her rum and cola as she made her way to the toilet.

"That's more like it," Jack said as he poured with familiar ease.

When she came out of the restroom, she saw a mountain of a man leaving the bar to find a place to sit in the back corner. She got her drink and watched as he glanced around. He looked right at her, she could swear it, and he kept staring. She downed her drink and ordered another, brushing off Jack's caution to take it easy.

She said to herself, "This must be my lucky night!" First, finding that her nest egg was ready to hatch, then the gorgeous guy eying her, she just knew he was the one to rock her socks off all night long.

She got a fresh drink, downed half of it and made her way toward his table. Positioning herself right in front of him, she asked, "Hi, Handsome! Buy me a drink?"

He scanned her from toes to head, and she felt chills when she saw his eyes. They looked completely black.

"Sorry," he told her, "but I'm about to leave." He moved his chair back and looked past her.

She followed his gaze to the bar and saw a young girl sitting there, drinking a beer and chatting with her friend. She recognized her as the girl from the grocery store. Beth something. Sharon knew the girl was young, probably half her age, and wondered why a man in his right mind would want that child when he could have a grown woman like herself.

She could not stifle the incredulous tone as she said, "Is that what you want? A little girl? Can't handle a real woman, huh?"

He looked her right in the eyes and narrowed his as he stood. She took a step back, not realizing just how tall and big he was. His voice took on a menacing sound as he leaned toward her and responded, "If I happen to see a," and making quotations in the air with his fingers, "'real' woman, I'll be able to handle her just fine!"

She felt a cold chill at not only the venom in his voice but the look she saw in his eyes and shivered involuntarily. As he walked away from her, she recovered her pride and yelled loud enough for everyone to hear, "I bet you couldn't even get it up for a real woman! Only little girls!" She started laughing at her victory, not noticing his hesitation, nor how his fist clenched before resuming his retreat out the door.

She went back to the bar and got another drink. A man beside her leaned over and said as seductively as he could manage, "I can handle a real woman!"

She appraised him and let him pay for her drink. He wasn't quite as tall as she was, and had a balding spot on the top of his head. He wore a tan blazer over a white shirt, a two-toned blue tie loosened and the top button of the shirt undone, with blue jeans and cowboy boots. He would do for what she wanted, but just until she could find someone else.

"So, where can we go to be alone?" he asked in a slight slur. She motioned to the men's room, and they headed into the back hallway together.

As the door shut, they collided together, frantically kissing and pulling each other's clothes open. When she tried to take him in, she found he was not ready, so she sank to her knees on the filthy floor and used her mouth. She felt him rise, then he shot unexpectedly. Unsatisfied, she turned and stormed out, leaving him breathing hard from his so-called exertion. A little later, when she saw him making his way toward the exit, he didn't even look at her.

She tried a couple of others, but by the time Jack bellowed "Last call!" she decided to just go home, pack some stuff and leave. She could at least make it to the next town and get a motel room.

Jack tossed the keys to the waitress to lock the door after Sharon, as she was the last one out. She had gotten him to let her use the restroom one last time, so she could splash some water on her face to revive a little.

When she got to her truck, she realized she had forgotten to tinkle while in there. She looked around, but only saw one vehicle in the lot; a nice old station wagon. It looked empty, and she had to go desperately, so she tossed her purse into the back of her truck and squatted. She thought she heard a noise, but knew she was alone. As she squeezed the last drops out and started to stand, everything went black.

Disrupted

I couldn't sleep. I arrived back at the motel a little past 3 A.M., took a shower and plopped onto the bed to try to get a couple of hours sleep, but the thoughts of things I could do to Sharon kept running through my mind.

After about half an hour of just lying there, the projectionist part of my brain loading scene after scene of ways to show her how useless she had become, I decided to just gather some things together and return to her. She had to be getting a little lonely by then, anyway, craving the attention of a man just as she obviously had her entire life. I intended to make sure she got that attention, even if it might not be the kind she wanted.

I grabbed my lantern and a change of clothes. Going through my tools, I found some pliers, a hammer, and a set of screwdrivers of various lengths and thickness. I also grabbed the machete in its nylon sheath. I did not have a definite set of plans for what I wanted to do, just wanted to experiment with a few ideas.

I loaded everything I thought I would need into the cargo bay of my station wagon and headed back to the old farm. When I passed the bar, I saw the truck still there, but no one around. At 4:00 in the morning, I figured the whole town, indeed the whole county, must be asleep. I pulled into the drive of the farm, went through the entering process, and drove toward the derelict house.

Before I got to the last turn, I turned the headlights off. I pushed the accelerator pedal gently after the curve, then shifted to neutral and killed the engine, coasting the final distance, and using the emergency brake to come to a stop. I didn't want noise or lights to announce my return.

Opening the car door, I could hear faint moans and muffled screams, though much weaker than before. It did not surprise me; I knew the stupid woman would not be still, nor would she have been able to take a nap waiting for me to return. She would have been tugging on her binds in a futile attempt at freeing herself, causing the wires to dig deeper into her flesh and leak some of her blood. I just hoped she hadn't done herself in before I could.

I got the light and a few of the tools from the rear seat floorboard and eased the door shut, still not making a sound.

As I entered, I aimed the beam of my flashlight at her and watched her eyes go wide with surprise, then a definite look of fear as she recognized me. The smell almost made me gag, as she had no choice but to piss and shit where she lay. Not like she could run to the potty when she needed to.

She began struggling harder in a last desperate attempt at breaking free, looking back and forth from me to her bindings.

I knelt by her side and placed my left hand on the

center of her chest as I put the light down and slid my right hand to the items I had in my back pocket.

"Shh, stop now," I near whispered to her. "You'll just cause yourself more pain." I had to feign concern to get her to stop thrashing about, but she still had that look of distrust. And fear. Still whimpering, her terrified gaze locked on my eyes and I smiled reassuringly, knowing she would feel a glimmer of hope that I might let her go.

"Here, let me help." I ran my left hand over her chest, along her collarbone, and up her left arm. Passing her elbow, I pulled out one of the four 10-inch screwdrivers. I stopped my hand at her bound wrist, pushed down hard to hold it still, and with all my strength drove the point of the tool through the middle of her hand, sinking it to the handle.

Her screams were beautiful to hear, but still a bit too loud. I moved my left hand to cover the gag in her mouth and eased the noise level a bit. Fresh tears and snot flowed down the sides of her face, her legs, and other arm thrashing and bouncing as far as the bindings would allow. When she calmed a bit and quit screaming bloody murder, at least for the moment, I stood and walked back out to my car and found some duct tape. I wouldn't be able to cover her mouth *and* hold her limbs down while I made use of the rest of the screwdrivers.

She kept trying to free her left hand but stopped when I came back in. She eyed me fearfully as I knelt at her right side, shaking her head when she saw the tape and repeating "no" through the rag. I pulled off my outer button-up shirt and used a corner to wipe the sweat from her jaw and chin, as the spit and mucus would impede the effectiveness of the tape. I pulled off a six-inch strip, then secured it snugly to her skin over the gag.

Her eyes widened again as I pulled another implement from my back pocket and held her right wrist with my right hand. She started bucking her hips, thrashing from side to side. I raised my right leg and straddled her waist to hold her still and completed the process of nailing her hand to the sod. Again, that glorious scream of pain and fear, this time much more bearable. Unfortunately, the scream stopped as she passed out.

I guess she had reached her pain threshold. I sighed with the realization that I would have to wait for her to recover before I moved on to the next stage. I passed the time by doing some exploring.

Across the drive, I walked up the path to the "big house." The steps and porch, while still mostly there, had some gaps of rotted wood, as did the inside floor. I shone the light around and up the stairs, but before I could go deeper, the noises from Sharon returned.

When I reentered, there were signs she had struggled. The flesh in her palms had torn more, and the pool of blood had grown.

"You really have a low pain threshold," I told her. "How am I going to have any fun if you keep passing out right as I get started?" She began shaking her head, almost violently, and crying from the pain and the expectation of more to come.

I decided to finish the task by driving the two remaining screwdrivers through her ankles, with her feet turned outward, piercing between the bone and the tendon. Needing to be more precise, I had to use my legs to press down on hers as I placed the tips and forced it through. She passed out again, causing me to take another break.

I sat back and surveyed that part of the job, then turned off the light and sparked a cigarette. After my eyes adjusted to the darkness, I went into the kitchen. The old appliances still sat where they had rusted away. Some dishes were in the sink, and the counters were covered by a thick layer of dust, dirt, and grime.

Looking out towards the tree line, I saw a light bouncing around. The events in the house were for me and the lady and required no audience. If the user of that beam heard any noise, an investigation would surely ensue. I needed to rid myself of that worry.

Stopping by my car on the way out, I pulled out my machete and slid it under my belt on my left hip, then went in search of my unwelcome visitors.

Jer and Tammy

Jeremy Barker had been down on his luck for a year. No matter how hard he tried, he just could not find work. Charity Falls, Utah, could not boast being the center of commerce by any means, so jobs were hard to come by.

He sat in the living room of the apartment he shared with his near life-long friend, Mike Manston, watching a movie on videotape. Well, not really watching it, just had it on for background noise. He had seen the flick countless times, but it was still his favorite of the 10 tapes they shared.

He busied himself with the task of cleaning stems and seeds out of some of the weed Mike had bought. Outside of making the meals and washing dishes, that was his main duty. They had agreed those chores were how Jer would earn his keep. Mike's job paid well enough to keep the bills paid and have just enough groceries to keep them from going hungry.

He finished rolling another joint and put it with the other ten. "*Fast Times at Ridgemont High*" played on, and right as Jeff Spicoli hit his head with his tennis shoe and said, "I'm so wasted," Mike burst through the door.

"Jer, get ready to go. We've been invited over to Beth's place for a party!" He hurried into the bathroom to take a quick shower and change his clothes. He didn't want to be smelly from busting his ass all afternoon when he got there.

Mike came back into the living room to find his friend still staring at the movie. "C'mon, dude! Turn that shit off!"

"We're really going to Beth's?" Jer jumped off the worn-out cushions of their old couch and stuffed some of the joints into his cigarette pack. "I thought you were just fucking with me."

As Jer hurried to shove his feet into his sneakers, Mike explained, "It's her birthday, and she wants to celebrate turning 21 and being able to legally buy beer by inviting select people to her party. She specifically told me she wants both of us there."

Jer looked at him, a bit of confusion showing, as he grabbed a couple of full packs of smokes. "Both of us?"

Beth Simpson had a reputation for being "hot-to-trot" with the guys they went to school with years ago. Mike had not really believed them. No way she could have done all the shit the Jocks kept saying without being all shove-it-in-your-face. Beth had denied ever doing anything with those guys. Mike believed her over them. Plus, he knew how they liked to make people believe they were such manly men that no girl could refuse. Mike really felt bad for Beth, as so many idiots did believe the lies.

"Yea, man," replied Mike as he shut down the TV and VCR, "and she said her little sister would be there, too!"

"Wait a minute!" Jer stopped in mid-stride and confronted his friend. "Her little sister is like, what, 12 years old?"

"Nah, man! She's about to turn 14, and Beth told me she's been dying to get her cherry popped! By you!"

"No, shit; 14, huh?" He handed the rest of the rolled weed and a full pack of smokes to Mike.

"Yep. And you know what they say, 'Old enough to bleed...'"

"'...old enough to breed!'" they finished together and contacted a high five, followed in one fluid motion by a low five and finished with a slap of palms pulled apart with fingers crooked and a snap. They headed out the door laughing and didn't bother locking it.

They were both 22 years old and were so similar in appearance that they could be mistaken for brothers. Mike stood maybe an inch taller than Jer and sported a thin, barely discernible mustache, while Jer only grew sparse hair on his chin. Both had brown, curly hair, and while Mike's eyes were hazel, Jer's were brown.

Jer offered, "Want to blow a doobie on the way?"

"Maybe half one." He pulled a joint out and lit it, as Jer lit a cigarette to help mask it.

The boys were in high spirits, laughing and joking as they walked the dark streets to get to Beth's house on the edge of town. When they got to the parking lot of the bar, they saw the old, blue pickup they knew belonged to Sharon Burlowski.

Mike looked at his watch, noting the time at 3:00 AM, and they agreed she must have found some prick to bounce on for the night. As they passed the truck, Jer instinctively looked through the window while Mike peered into the bed.

"Check it out, Jer," he called, "She left her purse here!"

"Dude, check it! See if she left us some cash!" Then, Jer noticed the pile of clothes. "Man, she must have stripped before going! What a fuckin' slut!" He moved the articles around and came up with the discarded thong panties. Pulling them to his face, he inhaled her musk. "Gah Dam! She must have been sopping wet! Smell these, dude!" He shoved the intimate apparel towards Mike, who slapped them away.

"Get that shit out of my face, man! What's wrong with you?" By this time, he had gone through most of the contents of the handbag. The wallet only had a twenty and three ones, which he had already pocketed. Suddenly, he found the plain white envelope. He pulled out the bulky container and looked inside, Jer right beside him.

"Holy shit!" they said in unison, and Mike began fingering the bills inside. When Jer tried to remove some, Mike crumpled it into his hand, grabbed Jer by the collar of his shirt and said, "Dude, she couldn't have earned this. She must have stolen it from the bank while she was working. Let's get out of here before someone sees us!" Then he bent, pulled up his pants leg and shoved the packet into his boot. "And not a word of this to anyone!"

Jer readily agreed and the pair took off at a run, continuing their route to the party. When they arrived at Beth's, the front door stood open and loud rock music issued from inside.

They walked in and Beth squealed from across the room, "Mike's here!" and ran over to them, launching herself onto him, followed by a searing kiss, shoving her tongue into his mouth, with one arm around his neck and the other hand combing through the back of his thick locks.

Jer witnessed this and thought to himself that his friend was a lucky bastard. As Beth peeled herself off Mike, she brought their attention to the young girl who had timidly followed her over.

"Guys, this is my little sister, Tammy. Tammy, this is Mike," as she locked arms with him to further stake her claim, "and this is his friend, Jer."

Jer looked the girl over. He had seen her before hanging around Beth but had forced himself to not actually notice her. Her being a little girl, he could get into a lot of trouble if someone even thought he looked at her in the wrong way.

At 4ft 3inches, she stood a little less than a foot and a half shorter than his 5ft 8in, and the sprinkling of freckles on her cheeks made her look adorable. He had doubts about her being as old as Mike said, no matter the efforts to make her look older.

She had straight black hair and like her sister, wore it loose, except for a pink hair band to keep it behind her ears. The rest cascaded down her back as far as her shoulder blades.

Her green eyes had little flakes of gold near the center, but she averted her gaze as if afraid of the appraisal Jer examined her with.

She wore a cute little pink crop top which served to accentuate her budding little breasts and showed off her tanned, flat belly and her "innie" belly button. On her slim hips, she sported a white denim mini-skirt extending maybe a quarter way down her shapely young thighs. On her dainty feet were a pair of bright, white sneakers atop white ankle socks with little pink balls at her heels.

In all, not a bad consolation prize, Jer thought as he stretched forth his hand in greeting. Tammy took it gingerly but acted like she didn't want to let it go.

Beth's own green eyes were sparkling as she looked up at Mike from her own 5'3" stance, and she bit her lip. She moved in between her sister and Jer, a storm threatening behind her eyes, and pushed her index finger up toward him. "You be a gentleman," she told him through clenched teeth. "If I find out you made her do anything she doesn't want, I'll cut off your balls and feed them to the dog. Then, I'll turn your ass in to the Police."

Jer agreed, saying, "I don't force myself on anyone, Beth. You think I'd really take advantage of her?"

Beth looked at her sister and back at the man she would entrust to take care of her. "Just be warned."

She brightened again and began pulling Mike by the arm deeper into the group of about 20 other young adults, telling her sister and Jer to have fun. Mike shot a wave over his shoulder, raising one eyebrow and winking, telling Jer silently to go for it.

Jer fidgeted a little, slightly embarrassed to be left with this pretty little girl. He stammered, "Got anything to drink?"

"Yea..." she whispered, slightly swinging side to side, "over there," nodding toward the kitchen. They were still loosely holding hands as she led him to the fridge. She pulled out two bottles of beer. Opening both, she handed him one and turned the other up, swallowing three gulps quickly and emitting a burp that would make a biker proud. She covered her mouth and flushed bright red, muttering, "Excuse me," and giggling self-consciously.

Jer developed a lopsided grin and said, "Nice!" He drank about half his bottle and belched himself. Tammy smiled and blushed again when he looked down at her, and she gently took his fingers and asked if he wanted to go sit on the swings in the yard for a while. He agreed, and they walked out the back door together to avoid the crowd.

They sat down and started swaying at the same pace. Jer reached into his pocket and pulled out a joint. "Do you mind?" She shook her head and watched intently as he lit it and took a big hit. While holding the smoke in, he offered it to her. "Want some?" as he let a small snort-cough.

He passed it over, watching as she experimentally put

it to her tiny pink lips and inhaled, followed immediately by a coughing fit as she passed it back and nearly dropped her beer. Jer couldn't help but laugh and she stood up, ready to walk away.

Jer snagged her hand before she made a step. "Hey, wait. I wasn't making fun of you." When she stopped and looked down at him she seemed about ready to shed tears, and not from the coughing fit. "Haven't you ever smoked weed?"

"No, I just wanted to try it," she told him. "I saw lots of other people doing it and just wanted to see what it was like." She spoke so softly, he almost couldn't hear her over the din inside.

"Do you want me to show you how?"

She looked at him to see if he just wanted to make fun of her, but only saw concern in his soft brown eyes. She felt a little twinge between her legs and nodded twice. He led her back to the swing seat and positioned himself on his knees in front of her to begin instructions. His position made his head level with hers, and he placed his hands on her kneecaps, holding her legs together.

He told her to first take a little smoke in her mouth, then open and pull a lot of air into her lungs with the smoke. As she followed instructions, he leaned back and sat on his heels, bringing his hands down to his thighs. She coughed again but considerably less.

"That's good, Tammy." She smiled at his praise making her pretty eyes glow. "This time," he said after taking a small hit, "when you feel that little tickle in your throat, try to swallow a little and see if that helps."

With each drag, she got a bit more control and she loosened up a little more, her legs stopped pressing as tightly together. By the time they finished the joint, Jer realized he could see up her skirt to her light blue panties.

When she noticed where he gazed, she pulled her legs together and playfully pushed at his shoulder, dissolving into a fit of laughter. He blushed at having been busted, then began laughing himself. Each time they nearly got control, they looked at each other and lost it again.

Tammy fell off the swing backward, rewarding Jer with a full view of her little panties, for she neglected to either pull her skirt back down or close her legs. He sat staring, still grinning like a fool, as she reached her hand toward her beer, wriggling her fingers in a grabbing motion.

He handed it to her and took a pull from his, still glancing from her eyes to her crotch. She stayed where she landed and began waving her bent knees toward and away from each other.

"You got a buzz?" he asked. She nodded and looked away as she brought her finger under her nose and began laughing again.

He crawled between her bent, raised knees and every time her laughter ebbed, he would gently prod her sides to get her going again. Jer did not want her laughter to stop. The musical sound tugged at his very soul, and he liked the feeling.

Finally, she told him she would pee if he didn't quit, so he moved off to the side to let her recover. Standing, she said she really did need to go to the bathroom and asked if he wanted another beer when she came back. With a silly smile still on his face, he could only nod. As she turned, he stopped her and brushed dirt and loose grass from her back, making sure to gently swat her little ass.

"Hey," she chided. Grabbing his hand to stop him, she looked toward the sliding glass door to make sure no one saw. "I'll be right back." She leaned down and pecked his lips and trotted off.

He longingly followed her slender form as she hurried to relieve herself. He had to reach between his own legs to rearrange himself.

"If she's 14," he mumbled to himself, "or anything-teen, then I'm the next Lotto winner! Still," he figured, "if she's willing, what's the harm?"

When Tammy came back, she had two beers, a blanket, and a flashlight. Jer had stayed in the same spot with one leg bent on the ground and the other up, his right hand perched on top of his upraised knee holding the cigarette he had lit, his left arm supporting him behind his back. She thought he looked like a dream as she moved to hold the blanket and the beers with the same arm, handed him the flashlight and extended her right hand to him, asking, "Can we go for a walk?"

Nodding, he took the light, then her hand as he feigned letting her help him to stand. They began strolling away from the house and the noise so they could be alone as they entwined their fingers, swinging their arms gently. Jer felt like a kid again; a giant kid, but younger than he'd felt in a while.

Neither said a thing as they meandered through the trees, but both were grinning and kept glancing at each other, their arms pressing together often in their stride. Jer couldn't understand his feelings. Hell, he was 22 and had been with several girls through the years. None of them had him feeling like Tammy did.

Tammy seemed different than the others somehow. He did want her, he just did not want to rush things. And not that he felt ashamed to be seen with her, even though he knew they had lied about her age, knew it when Mike told him. He felt he could proudly walk down Main Street with her on his arm and not care what anyone said. He would just be happy this beautiful little girl wanted to be with him.

They finally slowed and Jer announced he needed to

pee. He released her hand, set the light down and stepped behind a tree. As he did, Tammy put the beers down and began spreading the blanket at the base of another one.

Jer found he had to force his bladder to cooperate through his slightly tumid organ but finally managed to finish the process. He turned to find Tammy standing right behind him watching him tuck back in.

She handed him his beer and motioned him to sit with his back against the tree. He put the drink on the ground, did the same for hers, and took her hands gently into one of his. He used a crooked finger under her chin to raise her face to look at him and leaned down to tenderly touch his lips to hers.

They could feel each other's heartbeats pounding and bodies quivering as they pressed into each other. She had wrapped her arms tight around his neck, and he held her at the waist. He leaned back a little and stared into her eyes.

"Be truthful with me, Tammy; you aren't 14, are you?" He asked as delicately as he could to let her know that he knew, but didn't mind.

Still fearing he may walk away, she wanted to keep up the farce, but standing there looking into the depths of his eyes, she could not lie. She tried to look away, but he held her head still in the crook of his finger, silently encouraging her to answer.

"No," she admitted, then hope filled her pretty face as she said, "but I'll be 13 in two months!"

He smiled, grateful she trusted him enough to tell him the truth. Then, he kissed her full on the mouth, his tongue greeted by her eager acceptance. He backed away and took the position she had previously indicated.

"Thank you for being truthful with me," he told her, both of them grinning again. "Now, are you going to join me?" He sat with his legs bent up a little and held out both hands.

She straddled over him and lowered herself to sit on his lap. He lit another cigarette but made sure not to let the smoke flow into her face. She tried to take it, but he pulled it away.

"What are you doing? Aren't you a bit young to start smoking?" He had a mock look of disapproval.

Playing along, she said, "Oh, it's okay to let me drink beer, get me stoned and for you to stare at my panties, but not let me try a cigarette?" He blushed a little realizing how much trouble he could get in for what he'd done with her already. She placed her hand on the side of his face and turned his gaze back toward her. "Hey, I'm not going to get you in trouble." Her soothing voice calmed his rising fears.

She stood and backed away. Biting her lower lip, she began to undo the fastenings on the front of her short skirt. Jer watched with anticipation but thought he heard something in the bushes to his right. He grabbed the light and aimed it near where the sound came from and thought he saw movement. He called out to anyone who may have been there, "Hey, who's out there?" Tammy had gotten to her third button, but stopped and dropped next to him, following the beam as it cut the darkness, thinking someone had followed them, hoping to catch and ridicule them for wanting to have sex together.

"What is it?" she asked quietly.

"Nothing, I guess," he replied. "Thought I saw something move." He put the light down and patted her firm little backside, encouraging her to continue.

Interlopers

I crept into the woods towards the light. When I got close, I saw a young couple standing close to each other, a blanket on the ground with two beers sitting nearby. I could tell the guy was in his early twenties; maybe late teens, but I doubted that.

The girl, however, I thought could not even be in her teens yet. She had barely begun to develop and might have been on the brink of puberty. As I watched, the guy stepped up to her, took her face gently in his hands and pressed his lips to hers. She did not resist and even returned it, so I knew she was not being forced to do anything against her will. He said something to her and she replied, but she looked scared to say her piece. Then she brightened, and I heard faintly, "...but I turn 13 in two months!" Then he kissed her again.

He sat down on the blanket and took up his beer, saying something else in the process, and I watched as she lowered herself onto his lap. When he lit a cigarette, she tried to take it, but he seemed to rebuke her. They spoke a little more, then she stood and backed away a bit.

She began to undo her short skirt, slowly opening one button at a time. I moved a little closer, still not sure how I wanted to proceed, but the guy must have seen or heard me. He picked up the flashlight and pointed it in my direction. He aimed a little to the side of where I crouched, so I ducked behind a larger tree just before he scanned my position. When he turned it off, I looked out and saw her cuddled up to him. I was close enough now to hear her say, "What is it?" and his reply, "Nothing. Just thought I saw something. Go on, keep going."

The girl got back up and finished undoing her skirt. It fell to the ground revealing her little blue panties, and I had seen enough. I stepped out quickly, grabbing her long, soft black hair in my left hand and lifting her off the ground. She could not have weighed more than 75 pounds and was almost effortless to lift.

The guy reacted instantly, standing and rushing me as I brought up my right hand, caught him by the throat and lifted him as well, then shoved him back against the tree as I stepped forward. There just happened to be a broken branch there which found its way into the back of his skull and out through his eye.

The little girl thrashed and kicked at me, trying to connect with any part of my body she could reach. When the kid rushed me, she screamed, "Jer!" as I hoisted him into the air, too. When he connected with the branch, her scream was even louder. "NOOOOO!" Why are girl's screams so shrill?

I pulled the corpse off the hanger and let him slide to the ground before tossing her to his side. She huddled there, sobbing and calling his name incoherently. She looked up at me and opened her mouth to scream again, so I slapped her across the face and she slumped onto the body of 'Jer', unconscious. I looked at her, and there seemed something familiar, though I knew I could not have seen her before.

I picked up the dead guy and tossed him over my shoulder, ignoring the stench from the release of his organs. I picked her up around the waist and carried her under my arm, taking them both back to the cabin.

Big Boobs looked over as I entered, and showed more fear realizing I had two new visitors to join the party. She began shaking her head side to side as I laid the girl down, and her eyes went wider as I flopped the guy beside her and she saw the gaping hole where his eye used to be.

"I thought you might want a little company," I told her. She turned her head away, and I saw her stomach lurch. I pulled the tape from her mouth and the gag out, knowing she was going to vomit. The content was mostly acid as she hadn't had anything to eat for hours, and I knew it had to burn. When she finished, I stuffed the gag back in and re-taped her face.

I heard the youngster begin to stir, so I tied her wrists together to one of the poles and her feet to another. I hadn't planned for extra 'guests' so had to make do with what I already had going.

As the girl came to, she looked around trying to orient herself to the surroundings. I had to assume she had been here before as she had a look of recognition.

"Why am I here?" She was beginning to struggle with her bonds and realizing her predicament. "What do you want? Who are you?"

"If you don't want me to give you the same kind of kiss I gave her," I told the child while pointing at the cow, "then you better learn to keep quiet." She took the hint when she looked at the swollen face of her roommate, the fabric tied around her face and tape over that. She didn't try speaking but started crying again.

I moved the dead guy aside, leaning him against the wall. "There, now your boyfriend can watch, though I think he'll only see half of it. Get it? See half? He only has one eye left!" I began laughing as the two girls began trying to struggle again. I think they might have gotten the impression I was a little insane, but I knew exactly what I was doing. I figured those thoughts would be in my favor; as long as they reckoned I was crazy, the more likely they were to do as I told them.

I moved over to the young girl and squatted down next to her. "You don't want your boyfriend to see you bawling like this do you? He might think you're too young to take the next step with him."

She was staring at me with wide eyes, tears flowing freely from her green eyes. I could tell how pretty she was and knew she'd be a knockout when she got older. If she got older. The other one was looking up, glancing from me to the girl.

"You know, kiddo," I said to the child, "I just saved you." She got a quizzical look, so I continued, "Come on. You've seen the horror movies. Only the ones who drink, smoke pot, and engage in gratuitous sex die."

The older one began wriggling again, so I reached over and twisted the screwdriver in her hand a little, causing a muffled scream and more tears, but she quit moving around.

"Ah, listen to her screams. Don't you think they are just wonderful? I bet, when she had sex, she would scream out her little orgasms, even when she faked them." The girl had a confused look. "Oh, that's right, you don't know what an orgasm is, or how it feels. You were about to find out, though, weren't you?" I pointed a thumb at the dead guy. The girl began squirming and whimpering again, so I got up and went to the bag of goodies I had brought in from my car. Pulling out more duct tape and another screwdriver, I returned to my previous position.

She looked at me fearfully, and I confirmed her thoughts. "Yes, I will do to you as I did to her if you don't behave. You look more intelligent than she does," I nodded towards the one spread out, "and I'd hate to have to treat you like a common slut like her, even if you wanted to try to be like that."

"No, I didn't... I don't," she was trying to rationalize, but I cut her off.

"You were already drinking beer, I saw it on the ground. And," I added, "I could smell the pot smoke on you when I carried you over here."

"No, that was Jer! I swear I didn't. I only tried the beer because he asked me to!"

I ripped off a piece of tape and forced it over her mouth. "Do you think I'm stupid?" I yelled in her face. "I try to be nice to you and you lie to me!" I stood and began pacing back and forth, her crying again. I thought she was trying to apologize, but it was too late for that. "Damn, do all females think they can just spin out a lie and be believed? Do they think all men are idiots like this guy?" I kicked dead guy's foot, then returned to squatting beside 'Junior Miss'. She was shaking her head fast, crying and mumbling through the tape.

I grabbed her wrists, holding her hands together over her head and said as gently as I could, "I did not want this." I plunged the shaft through both of her tiny hands at the same time and pinned them to the ground. Her screams were different than the older ones', but oh, how they gave me the shivers.

When I opened my eyes, I saw she had passed out and I noticed she wet herself as well. I would not worry myself about that.

I stood and went back to my bag. Searching through it, I came out with my little wood saw. I held it up and looked at the older chick, relishing in the way fear gripped her all over again, then her slight relief when I shook my head and put it back. I looked some more and came out with a flat file. That might be interesting.

I approached her, holding the file behind me and smiling. She started shaking her head again, the fear back in her eyes, trying to pull her legs and hands free, but only getting pain. I stopped at her feet and knelt, taking her left ankle in hand and bringing the file out.

She tried to thrash around, oblivious to the tearing of her flesh, just trying to worm her way away from me as I placed it on the top of her foot and pulled hard. The skin tore away and her blood flowed. Her scream almost made its way around the gag, but I did not stop. I grabbed her other foot and repeated the process, this time pushing and pulling several times to get to the bone. She screamed and cried, then jerked so hard it tore the tendon around the shaft holding her down. That pain did the trick, and she passed out again.

I stood and wiped the sweat from my brow. Lighting a cig, I noticed the sun was about to rise, so went back into the kitchen to look out at the woods again. I saw more lights, maybe six, scanning the area close to where I got the kids from. I also heard shouting. I guessed they were looking for my new visitors because I heard them calling names, "Jer!" and "Tammy!" over and over.

Going back to the front door, I stopped at the two unconscious girls and said, "Tammy, huh? I'll be back with some friends of yours." She didn't respond, but I didn't care. I went out to get some more participants for the game.

Beth and Mike

Beth Simpson awoke on the morning of her 21st birthday in a glorious mood.

She had requested two days off several weeks ago as personal days. Since then she reminded her manager, Mr. Bane, at least twice a week that she would take them.

For four years, she worked at his store; she had not missed a single day without having a very good reason and calling him. She'd made sure he had plenty of time to get a replacement when she did.

Every time he needed her to work late, she made herself available. Her cash drawer always evened out, all the customers liked her, and she was always properly dressed. Mr. Bane had repeatedly praised her reliability.

The phone rang and Tammy, her little sister, came running into her room to give her the receiver. She could hear Mr. Bane huffing when she put it to her ear and knew he called to tell her someone had an emergency and he really needed her to cover. Again.

"I've tried everyone else I could think of, Beth," he whined, "please believe me. You are my last hope!"

She agreed, but only if he would pay her for the day off in addition to the hours she worked. He accepted without hesitation, thanking her profusely and promising to have her relieved as early as he could force someone else to come in. She knew him well enough to take him at his word, so she told him she'd be there by 2:00.

Not even bothering to get dressed, she went down to get her coffee and breakfast. To her utter surprise, Tammy already had a steaming cup of java and a huge western style omelet at her place at the table.

"Happy Birthday, Big Sis!" The young girl rushed to give her a tight hug and ushered her into the empty chair.

"Wow," Beth commented, "you did this for me?"

"Oh, Yea! Just to show how much I love you!"

Beth looked at her from the corner of her eyes with an eyebrow raised, knowing there were ulterior motives. Tammy always went all out when trying to bribe her sister.

"Uh-huh. I bet this has nothing to do with you wanting to stay here for my party instead of going to Julie Brooks' house like Mom and Dad told you."

Tammy diverted her eyes, looking guilty and blushing as she turned towards the sink to start cleaning the mess she made. "Well, you know they wouldn't find out, and I would stay out of the way and not bother anyone..."

Beth could tell a lost cause when she saw one. Tammy could always talk her way into things and really wasn't much of a pain. In fact, for a little sister, she wasn't that bad at all. Beth really liked having her around.

Beth asked through a mouthful of egg, "So, have you thought about someone for a date yet?" The tinkering sounds at the sink stopped and her response could barely be heard over the running water.

"Um, no..." The younger sibling turned the water off

and turned around. "Who are you asking?"

Beth put her fork down and swallowed, then took a drink of coffee. She looked the youngster in the eye and told her, "I'm going to force myself to ask Mike today."

Tammy's eyes lit up instantly. "Does that mean Jer will come, too?" The two girls had disclosed in secret that they respectively had crushes on the guys they named. Beth had wanted to be with Mike for a lot longer span of time, but when Tammy saw Jer for the first time, she fell for him just as hard.

"Well, they are best friends, and as close to brothers as two unrelated guys can be. So, I'd say, yes, if Mike agrees then Jer will probably be here, too. I just have to make myself bite the bullet, or neither of them will be coming."

Tammy turned back to her task, fazing into her own little dream world as Beth lapsed off into her memory while finishing her meal.

She remembered back to the 3rd grade. She sat in Home Room talking with her friends, Becca Solms and Jill Sanders. They were discussing boys, of course, and the topic always ended up circling around Pete Simms.

Though a year older than the three girls, they all thought him dreamy. Any time talk turned to boys, as it always ended up doing with those girls, Pete claimed the pinnacle.

Beth heard the classroom door open and instinctively looked toward it. The boy she saw come in made everything around her slow to a near stand-still. Conversation dulled in her ears as she watched him walk up to Mr. Jakes' desk and hand him his entry slip. Mr. Jakes looked at it, wrote in his attendance book, then scanned the room. The only desk open had been right next to Jeremy Barker.

Mr. Jakes called attention, "Class, I'd like to introduce Mike Manston. He's a new student here, and I hope you'll all make him welcome. Tell us where you're from, Mike?"

Beth could tell he was embarrassed as he muttered out, "We just moved here from Washington," and he hastily made for the chair indicated.

For the rest of the day, she couldn't think of anything else. Several teachers commented to her after classes about her uncharacteristic behavior, but the girl just gave a story about not feeling well. It didn't help that Mike had been placed in almost every class she had.

Years passed and the two never said much to one another outside of greetings in passing. Many times, Beth swore she saw him looking at her, but when she turned, he just walked away.

After they started High School, Pete Simms walked up to her and started a conversation. Suddenly, she felt like a grown up. An older guy, and Pete Simms, no less, was interested in her! Every day for weeks he would walk her to classes, save a place for her at the "Cool Kid's" lunch table and sometimes even walk her home.

The day came when he finally asked her on a date. She was thrilled! He picked her up in his Dad's car and they went to The Burger Joint, the popular hangout for the older kids. The entire time, she was show-boated around and she began to see that they were all phonies. She asked Pete to take her home after hearing some of them talk behind her back, so they left.

About half a mile from her house, he pulled to the side of the road and shut off the car.

She looked around nervously and asked, "Pete, what are you doing?"

"I just thought we could talk and, you know, just be alone for a while." He turned on the radio and scooted closer to her.

"OK," she said, "talk about what?" She did not feel right somehow.

He brought up his hand and brushed her silky black hair behind her ear and said, "You are so pretty, Beth. Don't you like me?"

She started feeling scared. He was much bigger than she, and if he wanted to, he could force her to do as he wished, which would probably mean she would end up getting hurt. She felt she had little choice but to let him have his way. She did not resist, but neither did she participate.

The next school day, everyone knew. Several of his friends had started asking her out, hoping they could get the same action. She refused to go with any of them, but according to what they told everyone else, she had met with them and done some pretty wild stuff.

At first, she tried telling people those boys were lying, but her words went unheard. She finally gave up, just biding her time until graduation.

She got a job at Mercer's Market, the local "get-it-all" store, and worked hard to learn everything she could. Though she liked to work the register, she knew how to stock, order, even fill out the end of day paperwork. Her figures were always accurate, and Mr. Bane gained complete trust in her.

Beth shook herself from her reverie. She had finished eating and still had to get dressed. Placing her dishes in the sink, she moseyed up the stairs while her little sister continued cleaning the downstairs rooms.

After her shower, she helped her sister pick out an outfit to wear, and reminded her to make sure to get some sleep during the day because the party would most likely last all night long.

She got to work about five minutes before she had to clock in. Mr. Bane called her into his office and told her he had Jason coming in early from the night crew to help out, but he couldn't show before 9:00. Beth told him that was fine and went to call Becca. They had plans to meet at Pop Inn for a couple of drinks before the party to celebrate the momentous occasion.

While on the phone, Becca told her that she would be bringing Pete as her date. With a huge sigh, Beth said it would be okay.

As she hung up, she saw Mike walk in the door. She stationed herself behind the register and went through her duties, watching to make sure he didn't leave. He got in line holding the sandwich he got from the deli for his lunch, along with a bag of chips and a six pack of sodas.

She greeted him as he laid his purchases on the counter. "So, I guess you're on your way back to work?" She felt nervous at the prospect of asking him to be her date, but she didn't want to miss this opportunity.

"Yea. Gotta work late, too," he replied. He seemed reluctant to talk to her, but honestly, he had always been intimidated by her. Ever since the first time he saw her, he felt she was out of his league. So many times, he wanted to ask her out, but always chickened out.

After she rang up his items, he turned to leave. "Wait, Mike," she blurted out. He stopped and turned to face her. She turned beet red as she forced herself to continue, "I'm having a party tonight, and I really want you to be my date."

"Really?" He perked up, thinking he might have misunderstood her. "You want me to be there? With you?"

"Well, yeah. I can understand if you don't want to..."

"Yes. I mean, I do." He crushed any doubts she may have and asked if they could talk about it during his break. He said he'd be by around five o'clock, but he would not get off work till around 11.

That settled, both went their separate ways, each smiling with a buoyancy in their steps. Beth's day flew by. Just before the time Mike had said he'd be back, she remembered she needed to ask Mr. Bane to cover the register so she could talk to him for a little while.

The two went to the back, and Beth threw her arms around his neck and kissed him. While talking, she revealed the truth about all the lies told about her, which he figured they had been. They also discovered a mutual attraction going on since that day in Mr. Jake's class all those years ago.

They both had to get back to work, so they agreed that Mike would come to her place after he picked up Jer. Beth asked if they could set his friend up with her sister, and explained why. After a brief discussion, they decided to tell Jer that Tammy was 14 so he'd be more willing to agree.

The rest of the day passed with no problems. Beth rushed home afterward to change for her meeting with Becca. Tammy hopped and squealed when she heard that both of the guys would be showing.

"I need you to get the house set up for me," Beth told her. "Jill and Billy will be here around 11:00. They'll be bringing the drinks, and I would like you to help however they want. I've already told them you would."

"Okay, don't worry. We'll be ready by midnight. That's when the others show, right?"

"Yep. I'll be here by one o'clock, and the boys probably won't be here till 2:30 or three. Can you hold out that long?"

Tammy assured her she had gotten plenty of sleep, and she'd be fine. Beth changed and rushed to the pub. Becca had just pulled up when she got there so they went in together.

They hopped up on a couple of stools and ordered a beer each. Though the bartender knew them, he said, "Are you two sure you're old enough? Let's see some I.D."

Both girls proudly pulled out their wallets and showed their identification. "Today's my birthday! I'm finally legal," Beth said with a giggle.

"Well, then the first one's on the house, girls." He leaned over and gave Beth a peck on the cheek. "Happy birthday, Beth."

"Hey! I didn't get that on my birthday last month," complained Becca. "What makes her so special?" She put on a fake pout, and the bartender hopped his chest onto the counter, grabbed her on both sides of her head and noisily gave her a kiss on her forehead.

Beth was laughing as her friend wiped the kiss off, saying, "Ewww! You can have that!" The bartender laughed as well, sliding them both a beer before walking away. The girls chatted about daily happenings until, behind them, they heard a woman yelling.

"I bet you couldn't even handle a real woman! Only little girls!" The two looked around, as did most everyone else in the bar, to see none other than Sharon Burlowski laughing at a huge man walking away from her. Beth noticed that he had his fist clenched tightly, and thought it would take either a brave or very foolish person to piss off a man that big.

The girls went back to their drinks and talk. Becca looked at the time, and told her friend, "Hey, we need to get back so we're not late for your party! Don't want Pete and Billy to have all the beer drank before we get there do you?"

When they got to Beth's house, Becca went off to find Pete while Beth looked for her sister.

"Hey, Squirt," she said. "You had any drinks yet?"

"No, Beth. I kind of wanted to wait for you and the boys to be here, that way, no one could say anything."

"Well, let's wait for them, then. We can mingle for a while until they show."

A half hour later, Mike and Jer came in the door. Beth had been watching for them and ran over squealing, "Mike's here!" Then she jumped on him, wrapping her arms and legs around him, and kissed him passionately. Tammy had followed her over at a more discreet pace and waited for introductions to be made.

After Beth introduced them all and gave Jer a stern warning about taking care of her little sister, she tugged Mike into the crowd, leaving Tammy and Jer to fend for themselves. An hour later, Beth looked around but did not see her little sister.

"Mike, do you think Tammy will be okay with Jer?"

He could see the concern in her eyes but knew his friend well enough. "Yeah," he told her, "Jer would not do anything bad to her. And he won't let anyone else hurt her, either."

Convinced, she whispered in his ear, "Let's slip up to my room." Giggling like school children getting away with something naughty, they ditched the party and went upstairs to be alone.

An hour later, lying next to each other, they were talking about how they had crushes on each other when Mike said, "I have something to tell you." He sat up and pulled on his pants, then reached into his boot and pulled out the envelope. Beth sat up and looked at him quizzically. "On our way over, we saw Sharon's truck still at the bar..."

"Well, that's not really surprising," Beth replied. She told him of the altercation she and Jill had witnessed at the bar. "She probably found someone to leave with after that."

"That's what Jer and I figured, but we also found her purse in the back, along with a pile of her clothes." Beth cut in saying maybe it was laundry, but Mike cut her off. "I went through her bag, and found this." He tossed her the package, and she gasped when she looked inside. "There has to be over a thousand dollars in there, probably more. No way she earned it." She nodded her agreement.

Her head jerked up at a noise outside. "Did you hear that?"

He could feel how tense she became. "Hear what? What's wrong?" He tried to calm her, but she got up and opened the window. Then he, too, heard a scream before it was cut short.

"Oh, shit!" She was putting on clothes hurriedly. "That was Tammy, I swear it!"

Mike was up in a flash putting the rest of his clothes on as well, and together they ran downstairs. Most of the people had gone. Becca, Pete, Jill, and Billy were the only ones still there. They all jumped up from the ruckus of the two running into the room.

"Beth, what's wrong?" Jill went to her friend's side, seeing the worry written on her face. In a few moments, Beth had explained the situation.

"Hey, maybe they're just playing a game," Pete said.

Beth turned on him, anger showing in her usually calm eyes. "Look, Pete! I should know my sister well enough to be able to tell a prank from panic!"

Before Pete could say something else, Billy stepped up and said, "Okay, so what do we do?"

"Just in case," Mike suggested, "we should find some weapons, anything that could cause damage."

Beth told Jill where to look for flashlights, then ran out of the room as Mike went to the front closet. Opening it, he found an aluminum baseball bat. He hefted it and took some practice swings, saying, "Oh, yeah! This will work!"

Pete rummaged around in the same closet and came out with a golf club. Taking it from him and tossing it back in, Billy chastised him, "Come on, Pete! Get serious, will you?"

Beth came back, showing what she went to get. Her father kept a .45 caliber pistol for emergencies.

Mike asked, "Did your Dad show you how to shoot

it?"

"Not really," she answered, "do any of you know how?"

Pete reached for it, but Mike pushed his hand away. "Pete, I've seen you throw rocks a couple of times. You couldn't hit something two feet in front of you."

Billy laughed and Pete punched him in the chest. "Like you could do any better!"

Jill returned carrying six flashlights. "They all seem to have good batteries."

Mike took the pistol as Beth found some bullets for it. He loaded the revolver and poured more ammo into his pockets. He had given the bat to Pete, and Billy found a machete outside the back door. The girls had armed themselves with kitchen knives, and each took a flashlight.

"It sounded like the screams came from the direction of the old Harris farm," Beth told them.

They headed out together, Mike leading with Beth behind him, holding his hand. Then came Jill and Billy, and finally Becca leading Pete. Calling for the missing couple, they advanced into the trees.

Fracas

I decided I needed to move my car. Sitting as it was in front of the building would be like a flashing neon sign saying, "Someone's here! Look inside here!" Without starting the engine, I put it in neutral and released the brake, pushing it onto the almost overgrown tire tracks until I felt it begin rolling on its own further into the property.

I rounded another curve and saw a drainage ditch slope down next to the driveway with a large weeping willow tree hiding the area. Deciding that would be the best place to hide the vehicle, I veered toward it. When the car got to the bottom, I reset the brake. That would do the trick. It would be out of eyesight from prying eyes, so I locked the doors and went to gather the new participants.

When I finally saw them, they were splitting up to search for the ones I didn't intend on letting them find. Groups of two, one guy and one girl each, moving in different directions.

The biggest boy, wearing a green jacket and blue

jeans, and a girl wearing purple spandex with a red jacket were going toward the house where the current participants were, so they had to be stopped first. I figured I would lead them off toward the main house and take care of them there.

I crept to the first bend in the road, away from the occupied building, and when I saw them come around the corner of the shack, I made a little noise and let the girl see my shadow. She grabbed the boy's elbow and pointed in my direction; he looked but didn't seem convinced. When he started steering her back toward the door, I picked up a rock and threw it, hitting him squarely in the back.

He turned and yelled out, "Who the hell threw that!"

Anger in his voice. Good, that's how I wanted him; angry and impulsive. He only held a bat, and I knew that would not pose much of a threat. As close as he would need to be to use it, the blow could not deter me. I shook the bush I hid behind and ran to another one closer to the main house but still out of their sight. I heard him running to the shrub, her behind him telling him to stop.

"Let's go get the others," she told him. That would have been the smart thing, and I was counting on him being brave, not smart. He did not disappoint.

"This fucker's gonna pay for hitting me with a rock!" The guy was serious, as was I. I rustled the next bush and made for the building. When I got to the corner, I made sure he saw me. "Hey! Stop!" He began chasing me. Excellent.

"Pete, stop," she called to him, but he kept after me and she trailed not far behind. "Pete, let's get the others!"

"Come on, Becca," he turned to her, pointing up the porch at the house. "He went in there. We have him now."

She reluctantly followed, clearly mad at him, but determined not to be left alone.

They entered the house and used the flashlights to pick their way across the rotted floor. I could see well enough in the half-light of predawn to make my way to the stairs. I went up, then pushed some debris over the side as they entered the foyer, almost hitting him. He cursed and ran up the stairs after me, leaving her at the bottom still calling for him to stop.

I moved into the first room off the landing and ducked behind a door that would not open all the way. He started being a little more cautious, brandishing the baseball bat like it was a sword.

Becca could still be faintly heard calling his name, but he was in search mode and would not answer her. He came into the room, pushing the door as far as it would go with the tip of the truncheon. I raised my fist, ready for his face. I saw his hand grip the edge of the door, relax a little and one finger at a time, re-grip it. He swung it out quickly, expecting to frighten anyone back there, but I knew what he had in mind and let my fist follow the swinging door to connect with his nose, causing a satisfying crunch of shattering cartilage and spray of sanguine fluid.

He hit the floor, shaking the landing, blood splattered from his sinuses across his cheeks. Becca's calls got softer after his yell and the thud. I could hear the quaver in her voice as she crept up the stairs to see if he was okay. I grabbed the bat and snuck back to once again hide behind the door.

When she got to the top she must have seen his legs in the doorway. I heard something metal hit the floor before she ran into the room and knelt beside him. The blood all over him made his situation look much worse than reality.

She acted hesitant to touch him, her hand getting close to the side of his face and backing off several times. I heard him groan as his head shifted slightly side to side. I stepped out and approached her back, bat raised. I hoped his vision would be clear enough to see.

He opened his eyes and blinked a couple of times, looking around until she came into focus. Then he saw me behind her and his eyes went wide. I raised the bat over my head looking directly into his eyes and smiling.

She expressed her relief that he was alive until she saw him looking over her shoulder with wide eyes. "What is it, Pete?" I could hear the fear returning to her voice. I waited for her to turn and see me, then swung down before she had a chance to issue the scream forming in her throat.

I saw her hair wrap around the aluminum and swore I heard the crunch of bone. As she collapsed, blood began to ooze from her ears and nose and her eyes rolled up. Her body crumpled and fell across his, pinning him to the floor.

I stepped over and nudged her off of him, then put my feet next to his elbows to reestablish his quiescence and patted the bat on my palm.

"Please," he begged, sobbing like a little girl. I loathed him for that; couldn't even face death like a man. "Don't... don't kill me, please!" He swayed his head side to side, making a poor effort to move away.

I hoisted the cudgel again and swung sideways, more like a golf swing than baseball, and made a solid connection with his left temple. His head jerked sideways, the hollow thunk sounding much like a grand-slam hit at the ballpark. I saw the base of his skull separate from his spine, the skin all that held it on.

I left them there for the moment. I had been away too long, and my 'hostesses' may have awakened. Taking up the knife that had been dropped, a long, serrated blade with two prongs on the tip, I went back to the cabin and heard noises inside, hushed tones of voices not wanting to be heard.

I held the knife at the ready and reached to push the door in just as it swung wide. Young Tammy had freed herself and was trying to leave, looking back at Sharon as she pulled the door. When she turned a squeal left her lips as she saw me. I thrust the blade down into her shoulder. She crumpled to her knees, looking down at her own blood flowing from her onto the floor, probably knowing she could be dying. The blade had enough length to have sliced her lung, evidenced by the gurgle as she collapsed.

Sharon screamed through the filthy gag still shoved in her mouth, and I knew that might bring someone else. As I approached her, she went quiet, but too late. "You stupid bitch!" I didn't yell but made my tone reflect my dissatisfaction. "You could have stopped her. You knew what would happen. She was only a child, gahdammit, and now she's bleeding to death because of you!"

Sharon shook her head back and forth as I stepped over her. Holding the bat just shy of the barrel, I let my grip slide down to the knob. I wanted to beat her senseless. Changing my mind, I went to exchange it for the hammer, then knelt next to her. I put my hand on her thigh and brought it down on her kneecap.

Damn! I forgot her secretions had lessened the adhesiveness of the tape on her mouth but got my hand over it before hitting her again. The third time, she passed out once more.

There were sounds of running feet getting closer. A male voice said, "It came from in there!" and a female replied, "Be careful, Billy!"

I stood and moved into the dark bedroom, withdrawing the machete I still had in my belt loop. The sun had made a full show and most of the living room was visible. I got behind the door and pulled it until it hit the wall, watching through the gap.

The boy pushed the front door open and immediately

saw Jer leaned against the wall, covered in blood and his face disfigured. As he cautiously edged in, the light fell on the two girls. His companion, upon seeing Jer, let out a gasp, then ran inside as soon as she saw the others.

"Jill!" He tried to stop her, but she had already knelt beside Tammy. I could hear him cursing under his breath as he quickly made it over to her and asked if they were still alive, eyes scanning the doorways and shadows.

"She's still breathing. Look what someone did to her. Stabbed her in her shoulder, and there are holes through her palms! Who could have done this?"

"I don't know, but they could still be here." His voice sounded more levelheaded than hers. He kept glancing around, searching the shadows for an ambush.

I let the door move just enough to let a short creak, which they both heard. He began approaching warily, machete raised above him.

I waited for him to get into the doorway and forced the barrier into him. As he stumbled back, I revealed myself, rushing out to catch him back-peddling to regain his balance. As I passed his girlfriend, I slashed down and cut her between a couple of her ribs. She fell over, her lungs gurgling as she drowned in her own blood. He saw her land on top of Tammy just as the guy regained his balance, his eyes going wide again as I swung my blade around to slice him, too.

His knife came up and connected with mine, his instincts obviously taking over before he noticed I had gotten so close. We danced around, each swinging to get the better of the other, as we stepped over the bodies on the ground.

One of his attacks glanced off to the side and sliced into my forearm. I saw him smile as he drew first blood, but my adrenaline flowed thick enough that I didn't even feel it. I took advantage of his pause and hacked into his thigh, catching the artery and sending him to the ground with a yell of pain to bleed to death.

I needed to complete the tasks and get the hell away from there as soon as possible. Too much activity to stretch out my retribution and the parents of the young ones could come looking any time. I knew there were two more in search of me already and that they also needed to be taken care of so I would have more time to get away. But first, the captive I had originally sought to be the only player in the game had to be finished off.

Fickle fate decided to favor me again, for when I flung the dripping blood from my machete, I heard Sharon begin her muffled screaming anew. She had seen me stab the youngster earlier and probably saw the new additions who died during her unconscious period. No matter, I wanted her to be awake when I did her in anyway.

First, I needed to reapply the muffler to quiet her noise maker. That done, I went to my pile of tools and rummaged around, coming up with a utility knife. I looked right at her wide eyes and jiggled my eyebrows up and down as I slid the razor out full length, then backed it down to just the sharp tip as I knelt next to her.

"I'll not lie like doctors do by telling you this won't hurt a bit. It's gonna hurt like hell." I let the grin show again as her tears began flowing anew.

I started just above her shattered knee, pressing the tip in just enough to penetrate the layers of skin as I pulled toward me. She jerked her leg back and forth, up and down, causing the blade to swerve and make a crooked cut. Continuing up past her hip and circling her navel, I kept continuous pressure. I stopped when I reached her chest.

"Now, let's see about taking off some of that flab you like to think makes you desirable," I told her. I made a slow presentation of extending the blade the rest of the way out.

Estimating where the sides of her ribs lay, I jammed the point hard into the side of her saggy breast. In a sawing motion, I cut her left tit off, then did the same to the right. She had bled so much through the night, plus what ran out during this session, she had little strength left to fight anymore. Kind of ruined the thrill of the process.

For the final act, I untied her left hand and moved her arm to lay to the side, then took up the machete and brought it down as hard as I could on her neck, severing flesh and cartilage. I had obviously cut in between her neck bones that would have been the only thing holding her together, for her head rolled away amidst the final spurts of blood.

I stood and went to the body of Jer, where I used a less messy part of his jeans to wipe most of the gore from the blade. Then, I went to Billy's corpse and ripped his shirt off to wrap around the cut he had made on my arm.

It was time to get all the bodies together and leave this place.

Confrontation

Mike had heard faint yells and screams. He led Beth by the hand, pistol held in his left hand in front of him, pointing it at the ground as they rounded a curve in the overgrown path.

The sun glinted off something in the ditch behind some low-hanging branches. They went toward it and found an older model station wagon. They could tell it didn't belong, for it looked brand new and the farm had been abandoned for a decade or more.

"This isn't good," Mike whispered. He tried to look through the windows, but they were tinted too dark to see in.

Beth looked around and found a large rock, intent on smashing the glass, but Mike stopped her. "Whoever owns this is probably nearby and more than likely the one causing people to scream. If you break that, you will broadcast our position."

She nodded and dropped the stone. They continued toward the sounds, making sure to stay off the driveway.

As they reached the crest, they saw a huge man exiting a dilapidated house, the early morning sun sparkling off the blade at his side. They could see a cloth tied around his left forearm, blood seeping through.

Beth whispered, "That's the big guy from the bar. The one Sharon hollered at last night. What's he doing here?"

"Nothing good, I bet."

When the man disappeared behind some bushes heading toward the big house, the young people edged out to follow him.

"What if there's someone in there that needs help?" Beth asked, pointing at the building the stranger came out of.

"I'm betting, if anyone is in there, they are probably beyond help," Mike replied. "I don't want either of us to see what he's been up to yet. We need to stay focused. Whatever, or whoever he left in there would distract us."

Reluctantly, Beth nodded and followed, though she would have rather gone to see if Tammy had been taken there. They skirted the overgrown hedge and made it to the back door since the mystery man went through the front.

The door stood ajar, but not enough to squeeze through. As Beth reached for it, Mike put his hand on her arm.

"Those hinges are rusted," he said. "They won't swing easily. When they break loose, they'll squeal like a stuck pig."

"So, what do we do?" She almost sounded exasperated by his continuing circumspection.

"Come on." He led her across the porch, picking his way carefully to avoid the rotted boards. At the end of the platform, they found a window that had been completely shattered and decided that would be their point of entry.

"Just watch your step. We have to be as quiet as

possible," he spoke in a breathy voice.

"Okay," she whispered back.

Once inside, they paused to allow their eyes to adjust, then continued toward the stairs. Mike had slid the pistol into the back of his pants waistline to free his hands during their entry, so decided to leave it there for the time being.

There were faint noises of shuffling coming from up top; something being dragged, possibly. Mike could feel his palms start sweating and wiped them on his jeans. When he looked at Beth, he could see a vein in her temple throbbing and knew she felt as much fear as he did.

A grunt drifted down to them that sounded female. They looked at each other, and Mike held a finger to his lips.

"What are you doing?" The girl's voice above them asked. "What do you want?"

The Beth and Mike heard a deep voice mumble a reply, but could not make it out.

"But, why? What did we do to you?"

Mike tried to use the conversation as a cover for his movements. He studied each tread to make sure they wouldn't creak, and the two made their way up.

They heard a scream and rushed up the rest of the stairs. The whimpers stopped as they peered around the corner into the long hallway off the landing, leading to the bedrooms.

Mike pressed his back against the wall next to the corner, Beth next to him. She placed a hand on his upper arm and mouthed, 'Be careful' when he looked at her.

He nodded his agreement and reached behind him to make sure he still had the pistol.

He looked back around just as the big man backed out of the room, his hands full with a pair of dainty feet. They both jerked at the surprise. The man dropped the ankles he held, and Mike instinctively pushed Beth away as he lunged at the intruder.

The sudden attack had its effectiveness and they both hit the floor.

The gun fell out of Mike's waistline while the man's machete cut his belt and flopped to the side, as well. They wrestled around, Mike trying hard to keep an advantage.

The scuffle brought them to the broken railing, Mike still holding his position on top. He pressed the man's head back as it cleared the edge. With his teeth clenched tight, he put all his effort into trying to keep it there while holding the man's arms in the crook of his elbow, but the big guy had more strength and forced his gaze to the youngster that had him pinned.

When their eyes locked, Mike let him go, leaping up and backing quickly. The man had pitch black eyes, the pupils seemed to burn a fiery red. He had never seen eyes that looked so evil before.

"What the hell?"

The big man slowly rose, bending his head to each side with popping noises of his neck bones. He had a slight grin as he popped his knuckles as well. "At last, an opponent with guts."

As Mike backed even with the doorway they started at, he saw Becca stretched prone inside, her face covered in blood. It looked as though she had been thrown in a huge washing machine on spin cycle with a load of razors. Cuts lined her face and her head looked as if it had been used for batting practice. Further in, he saw Pete laying on his back, his head at a most unnatural angle. Mike knew they were both dead.

He looked back at the man, confusion in his eyes. "Why? Why did you kill them?"

The man still had the grin as he glanced at the two bodies, then at Beth and, finally, back at his adversary.

"You kids should have stayed away," he said evenly. "Had you done so, I would have finished with what I needed to do and been gone long ago."

"What you had to do? What does that mean? What's it got to do with my friends?"

The big man just shrugged and shook his head. "Doesn't matter," he said, his lips curling into a sinister sneer. "You unfortunates will be dead soon and I'll be gone from this... I guess you call this a town."

"You won't be gone. Not if I can help it," Mike told him.

The large man laughed without humor causing the sound to be more unsettling than the random violence he doled out.

"Oh, and I suppose you're going to stop me?"

With that, Mike lowered his head and grinned. "No, not me. Her." He pointed behind the invader, who turned to see Beth standing with the pistol held in both hands, training it directly at his head.

"Don't. Move," she commanded.

He looked back at Mike, the same grin he'd had since rising from the scuffle. "So, she'll shoot me, huh?"

Mike had removed himself from the line of fire, in case the man could move fast enough to avoid the bullet, so he didn't get hit instead.

With lightning quickness, the man dropped and swung his long leg around backward, knocking Beth's feet from under her as the gun flew out of her hand. When she hit the floor, a solid thunk from her head contacting the landing sounded and she lost consciousness.

The pistol landed on the floor at the feet of Becca's corpse, directly between the two men who once again faced each other. They both glanced at it, then back to look into the eyes of their foe.

Mike made the first move, but not toward the weapon.

He bent his arms and lunged at the killer, hitting him in the torso with his shoulder as a football player would tackle a running back. The sudden move came as a surprise to the killer and they both hit the floor again. Mike pressed his advantage and began reigning punches against his target, hitting anywhere he could in attempt to overpower him.

Flailing arms from both men met and deflected blows. The large man thrust his arm up, hitting Mike full in the sternum. The force of the contact pushed him up and off, his feet back peddling to try to get his balance.

Tripping on the prone legs of Becca's body, he fell into the room and landed facing her. He saw the handle of another knife embedded in her shoulder at the base of her neck, having been thrust down into her torso.

Mike emitted a yell and tried to roll away, his hand landing on and closing around the grip of the pistol. The killer had gained his feet and rushed into Mike's back, forcing them both further into the room. They landed hard on the floor and skidded into to the body of Pete.

Mike reached around behind him with his empty hand and grabbed a fist full of hair, using it as leverage to pull himself around to face his attacker. The man raised his huge fist above his head, ready to pound the life out of Mike, who brought the pistol up to the man's diaphragm and pulled the trigger.

The blast, though slightly muffled by being against an obstacle, startled both men. Time seemed to stop for a split second, then the man brought his hand to the wound. When he looked down and moved his hand, they both saw the black blood dripping off.

The madman gave a half grin and snort. "You've killed me," he said. He leaned forward onto his other hand and rolled to the side. As a full grin emerged and blood formed on his lips, he looked Mike in the eyes and said, "You've killed me. What's mine is now yours," as his head fell to the floor.

With his last breath, a translucent black mist emitted from his mouth and nose, hovering between the two. Mike tried to back away as he rose from the floor, but the mist enveloped him, causing him to breathe it in. He fell unconscious to the floor.

He woke to Beth shaking him by the shoulder. "Mike! Mike, are you okay?"

He felt groggy, aches and pains throughout his body as he came to. He sat up with her help and felt her urging him upright to stand.

"Come on, let's get back to the house. We need to get you to the hospital."

As they made it to the doorway, Mike stopped and looked behind him to the lifeless body of the man who wrought such destruction.

"Wait," he said and shuffled his way back to the body.

"What are you doing?" She just wanted to leave. The stench of death from the trio of corpses permeated the room.

"He said what was his is now mine, so I'm claiming it." He knelt and patted around until he found the keys for the car, then fished them out and pushed them into his own pocket.

They made their way back outside and through the woods to Beth's house, neither saying a word. Beth had an arm around his waist and her hand gripped his elbow to give him support. Mike could only hug his abdomen and let her lead his steps.

When they got to her house, the sun had neared its apex. She took him upstairs and laid him gently on her bed, then went to get a large bowl of warm water and a cloth to clean him up.

"Get some rest. I have to call the cops to report this," Beth told him. His eyes closed as he dropped into a dreamless sleep.

When his eyes popped open he found himself on Beth's bed alone. He swung his legs off the side and cupped his head in his hands even though the pains seemed mostly gone.

His boots were on the floor next to him, the envelope of money on the nightstand. He pulled the boots on but left the money there. He wouldn't need it. He knew, if Sharon's truck still sat in the lot, he would have enough without it.

As he made his way down the stairs, he heard Beth talking to the police. "That's all I know. We saw him dragging Becca by the ankles, and then the confrontation started. I got the gun, but he knocked me down, and I hit my head.

"When I came to, they were in the room, the big guy shot in the gut and Mike unconscious next to him. I shook him awake and we came back here. I cleaned him up a little before he went to sleep, then I called 911."

The talk faded as Mike made his way to the back door and outside. He had to get going before they caused more inconveniences.

When he got to the station wagon, he drove off the property just in time to see several police cruisers pass and pull into the driveway he just left.

He went back to the bar. Sharon's truck still sat in the same spot and others were scattered around the dirt lot. He pulled up beside it but found the door locked. In the bed, he took up her discarded shirt and used it to hold the tire iron to smash the window. Sure enough, three envelopes stuffed with bills were in the glove box. He took them, got back into the car, and drove away.

As he exited, he saw another police cruiser pull in and stop next to the truck. He smiled as he left them to do their work.

At the hotel, he went into the room and gathered up everything that didn't belong and loaded the car back up.

Then drove South out of town.

He glanced into the mirror and ran his fingers through his curly brown hair. His eyes had gone black, a slight red glow glimmered for his pupils, and he smiled again.

His next adventure would play out a little more smoothly, now that he had a little experience.

Hell Endures

Vanish

I left Utah behind, as well as the form I had grown accustomed to. As I drove, I could not help but reminisce about the situations that brought me to that point.

Mike had become the third body to host me after defeating Joel. Not that any of the people I've been in had a choice, for once inside, I could control them completely as well as access every memory in their heads. Even if they could not consciously bring the memory to mind.

With the initial one, a female, I learned that some of the males have more natural strength. I later discovered the men didn't need to be bigger, for Mike did not have the same stature as Joel but won that battle.

My first conscious thought informed me I needed to use a person, so I entered the closest one. I instinctively knew that, once in, the only way to be released came with the death of whoever I inhabited. I had a feeling if I stayed in the body after the demise of my host, it would be my end, as well.

Allie Makeland had proved a valuable initiatory puppet. As soon as I invaded her, I delved into her brain, absorbing all the information I could find. I didn't drain the mind, for I knew the best way to go unnoticed would be to make it look like nothing had happened. I learned in an instant everything she knew, whether she remembered it or not.

She had a thirst for understanding that even she didn't know about. From her youngest childhood memories, if she could not get the information she wanted, she would keep searching, asking adults and, after she learned how, reading book after book to find out more. Most of what she heard or read quickly found its way out of her mind. She only wanted to know the answer, not everything to do with the subject.

However, everything she had looked at had been stored in her memories and I assimilated it all. As it turned out, because of her small stature, providing information had been all she could do for me; she didn't have the strength or proportions for more physical endeavors.

When Joel came into the picture, I saw an opportunity. I needed to take the man as host, which meant getting him to kill Allie. That turned out not being too difficult, after all.

Joel Jones had an immense size. Standing six-and-a-half-feet and weighing over two hundred pounds, he dwarfed her diminutive 5' 1", hundred-pound frame. His physique showed that he had the strength I would need, as anyone could see at first sight his veritable lack of flab.

When the time felt right, I got her to make a date with him, to rendezvous at a secluded spot. When they met, I began to manipulate my next target into the precise mood needed. Desire led to the most violent reactions when spurned.

I engaged him in a conversation, learning about him and giving bits of information regarding her beliefs and past. I chose what to reveal carefully, keeping everything near what he told me.

We met several times, over dinner at a Diner, or drinks at a local bar. I had the information from all of Allie's previous relationships, every little nuance, to know just how to manipulate the man into deep feelings for her. When he got to the level of desire I needed him to be in, I would suddenly change my mind and scorn him into a rage.

When the time felt right, I suggested we hook up at a remote spot I had discovered so we could be alone. I gathered the stores to lay a romantic picnic, complete with wine. We sat next to each other watching nature play out before us, sitting close enough to softly brush skin against skin with just the right movements, coyly glancing at each other while I sent him all the signals so he'd think he was about to get lucky.

I led his emotions with ease, going through just the right actions that would get him sexually excited. Kissing ensued and quickly led to fondling. When he started moving his hand up my thigh, I sensed the time had come.

"No!" I pushed his hand away and scurried from under him. "That's not what I wanted," I said, backing from him. "I can't believe you thought I would just have sex with you, outside and exposed." I made my voice rise in pitch and volume with each admonishment.

Flummoxed, he looked around to see if anyone noticed, even though we had chosen the location for its complete seclusion. I laughed at his confusion, pointing and chiding his lack of understanding.

I could see him getting more angered than confused,

embarrassment replaced by ire. He stood and turned to walk away, but I pressed on and ran up behind him, dainty fists beating ineffectually on the brick wall serving as his back.

He turned just as I swung and it caught him in the diaphragm. The blow knocked some of his breath out, as I had used more force than the small body could have managed. I watched his eyes turn red, his rage clouding out reason. The time had come.

"What, you can't handle getting hit by a little thing like me?" I sneered as I pointed at his manhood, laughing, and said "Even for as tiny as I am, at least I'm bigger than you."

That tipped him over the edge. He raised a huge fist, his brow crinkling and his other hand snatching the top of my shirt. Not saying anything, his blow surged forth and broke my jaw. As I looked up through the tears, I saw another strike heading toward my face. I took it full force, feeling the life begin to dwindle.

"You have killed me," I declared, voice distorted by the gurgle of blood. "What's mine is now yours."

I watched as his eyes followed me escaping her with her last breath. He dropped the lifeless body, backing slow, unsteady, hoping to get far enough away to feel safe. I rushed into his face and entered the same as I did Allie.

I secured his mind in short order. Everything he knew I added to what I learned from her.

The change in altitude came as a little shock at first, but I adapted without much problem.

Looking down on the corpse I just vacated, I felt a twinge of want, a desire for her tiny body, plus a small sense of regret.

Some of the sexual feelings were remembered, recalled from his short-term memory of the make-out session. But there were thoughts of other females from the past, too. Deep-set memories of many encounters with girls that, while sexy entirely dressed, turned out not being very attractive in the nude.

He had many times observed how various women would stuff themselves into clothes they had already grown out of, some of whom seemed to think they were the hottest thing around, that every man should want them. They acted like any that didn't desire them must be gay, or in need of psychological help.

I had to shake myself from the musings and vacate the premises. With no clear idea of where to go, I instinctively knew there had to be some purpose for my presence. The time had come to go find that purpose.

I opted to keep the vehicle I acquired while in the girl. A classic, mid-sized coupe, mid-seventies era, dark blue with metallic flakes. The car Joel arrived in had too many problems, and I needed something with trade-in value. I couldn't keep either one, as they could be traced.

I didn't bother with trying to hide her body. By all evidence, there had been few, if any, visitors there for a very long time. She wouldn't be found anytime soon.

Giving one last glance back, I felt another pang of regret that I had to eliminate such a fine creature.

I needed to vacate the Idaho area, for I felt the need to migrate. I hit the State Highway, headed south and into Utah.

I got fortunate enough to pass a car lot with a wide variety of vehicles from recent years, as well as a select inventory of classics.

When I pulled in, the salesman walked out, hands wringing, almost salivating over the coupe. I had hoped Allie's car would be desirable, for it would make the transaction much easier.

"Ah, beautiful restoration you have there, Friend." His smile dripped with saccharine. "I'm hoping, as you turned around to come in, that you have some business you wish to discuss?" His eyes, through his introduction and the handshake, remained on the car, taking in every line, every shiny surface. It may have been covered in dirt, but one could still see the pristine nature of the body.

I popped the hood for him, and he marveled even more. A Hemi had been stuffed into the bay, adorned with chrome headers, valve covers, air cleaner, and thermostat housing. No oil blow-back, nor surface rust anywhere on the body or undercarriage.

"A true beauty to behold," he whispered.

"How about you show me what you have?" I had to snap him out of his reverie. I really didn't want to spend too much time there.

He led me into his showroom, and I took my turn to marvel at the beauty. He had 10 classics, American, British, and German. No kind of theme between the vehicles, just excellent examples of decades gone by.

The memories I had access to, the combined knowledge of Allie and Joel, spanned enough overlapping years to make a fine decision, trading the muscle car for a beautiful Station Wagon, with wooden panels on the sides and windows tinted dark enough that one couldn't even see inside in broad daylight.

I had the ability to write with Allie's fancy script, so had signed the title she kept in the glove box over to Joel. I convinced the salesman that we had just made the transaction and didn't have time to find a notary to do it properly. It turned out not being too hard to convince him, for the guy really wanted the old blue car. I had a feeling it would spend more time being driven by him than sitting in the shop waiting for someone to buy it.

I kept heading south. Almost six hours later, I neared the southern border and needed a rest period. The next town I hit, I passed the bar where Sharon came into the picture.

After that fiasco, I realized the need to use a more erratic route while keeping my eyes out for another prospect to experiment on at each stop I made. I liked the feelings that coursed through me during the torture of Sharon, as well as how her screams excited me, and wondered if someone else would give the same. I intended to find out.

At least I knew I could, when necessary, switch hosts so I wouldn't leave any witnesses. That would aid in confusing any law enforcement who might try to track my activities.

With the money I had gotten out of Sharon's truck, I wouldn't have any worries about coming up short financially. I did need to get rid of the wagon, as it, and I in it, could be recognized from a description by Beth.

While travelling through Arizona, I reached a turnoff going into the National Park and decided to see what sights it offered. The roadway twisted and turned through hilly terrain with sparse vegetation and over bridges spanning the mostly dried creeks. The route meandered West toward Nevada.

I passed a large ranch bordered on the backside by a deep ravine. A nice wood beam fence stretched a good mile along the roadway. On the side of the entrance, they had a late Seventies all-terrain vehicle set out for sale. Maybe they would be willing to trade for the wagon, plus offer a bit of cash to cover the difference. The 4-wheel drive didn't have as much resale value, even though it looked to be in decent shape, as it wouldn't have the same amenities.

I pulled in and drove up to the house. An elderly fellow came out to greet me. He couldn't pull his eyes away from the fine example of a bygone era.

"What a classic," he told me. "You don't see many old cars like that running around anymore, at least not in that good a shape."

He and I bantered for a while, with him reminiscing that he used to have an old station wagon, and missed the room they offered. I knew I could get the deal.

We traded off vehicles, plus he gave me a bit more cash than I anticipated. After we signed the papers, I moved my belongings from one to the other and continued my journey.

When I crossed the border into Nevada, I found a smaller highway that led northwest and followed the curvy road for several hours before finding a town containing a half decent motel.

Pulling in, I stepped into the office and rang the little bell. The manager, bent with age and arthritis, shuffled from the back room to greet me.

"Don't git much reg'lar business 'round these parts," he told me during the transaction. "We just vacuum ev'r coupl'a days. Give th' customers what they need, let 'em fend fer th'mselves. That's how the prices stay low."

"I would like to be as far from the road as possible," I said. "The noise of traffic keeps me awake." I paid him, got the key and linens, and drove to the end of the long building.

The room wouldn't win any awards, but they kept it clean and in good repair. A double bed, a nightstand with a little lamp and a four-drawer dresser were the only furnishings in the main room. No phone, which I didn't need anyway.

The bathroom sat off to the left toward the back of the space, I figured it mirrored the room next door so they could share plumbing. As an added amenity, they had a small fridge next to a counter on which a two-burner electric plate had been installed. I doubted I'd need all those, as I just needed to rest long enough to get back on the road.

I placed the linens on the bed and prepared to take a shower. I hadn't had one since the confrontation that led me to be in Mike's body and knew from the time driving in the hot sun that I smelled none too fresh. I probably would have smelled worse had I still been in Joel.

After the shower, I made the bed and got some sleep.

In the morning, I stripped the bed and left all the used linens in a pile to make it easier for the maid. When I turned in the key I asked directions to the nearest restaurant for some breakfast.

I continued traveling west until I after I made it through Nevada and into California. Turning South at the next interchange, I started looking for a place to find a new victim. The idea of a fresh body to work on gave me a slight thrill.

I began passing more elaborate property fences. Well established, expensive workings set back from the usual Government Easement measurements. A couple looked brand new, with another still in the building stage. The houses were built between the scattered hills and mountains, most of them far enough away from the road to afford privacy and near eliminate all but the worst highway sounds.

At the base of the next mountain range rested a cozy little residential area opposite a huge casino. The gambling house, identified as "Cody Bills" by the myriad of signage, had a huge outdoor video screen flashing all the amenities contained therein. I felt sure the houses and apartments were for the many workers.

I continued past with the mind to return to see what else it might offer. Through the pass, I entered a town named Branson. Still upscale compared to the burg I found the night before, but not as grand as the mansions East of the casino.

I located a motel on the edge of town and once again took several items into the room. After cleaning up, I climbed back into my truck and went in search of a viable candidate.

Back at the casino campus, I drove around the buildings to get an idea of where certain entrances and shops were.

I saw behind the main building, set off about a quarter mile, a sign for "Danse Club," and figured that would be a good possibility.

I drove through the almost empty parking lot, a few cars parked in the far lot but most of the patrons preferred to be closer to the building. I went to the back lot and found a spot to park somewhat near to the entrance.

Inside, I found my usual preference in a corner table, though all the booths were side by side, so I couldn't be as secluded as I liked.

With the nearest speaker directly over my head, the noise didn't slap me as it did when I crossed the dance floor. The music blasted through the rest of the large room, the center tables and chairs ringing a big dance floor seeming not so wise a choice for conversing.

When the young lady came by to get my order, she hesitated just a bit. I had to concentrate on taking some of the blackness out of my eyes so as not to make people too uncomfortable.

"Just bring me a bottled beer," I told her, "and a fresh one when I'm almost out." I slid a one-hundred-dollar bill onto the table for emphasis, and she scuttled off to get my drink. When she returned, I asked about the seeming emptiness of the joint.

"Oh, it'll pick up in just a little bit." She seemed to be filled with nervous anticipation. "Saturday and Sunday nights are always hopping around here."

True to her statement, people started trickling through the doors not long after. Couples and groups came in with boisterous abandon, some stopping at the bar for their drinks, others migrating around to stake a claim on their favorite tables. A few found their way directly to the dance floor, starting their gyrating and hopping about to the pulsing beat.

A group came in, a bit older than most of the others, and commandeered the table next to me. There were nine, 5 men and 4 women. I sensed there would be another.

I saw her walk in. Almost as if everything else faded and she remained in stark clarity. She had a bit of extra weight and looked as if she usually got what she wanted.

She approached the table next to mine. "Wriley," her friends called, greetings and chides rebounding as she took her place. They bantered loud enough to be heard over the noise, which carried clearly over to me, as well.

"Hey, Wriley," one guy sitting across from her called. "How goes your efforts to glean more cash from the Powers That Be?"

"I just can't convince them," Wriley responded. "I must be losing my touch, nothing I've tried works."

They all took turns asking if she tried various methods of persuasion, to which she either acknowledged or glared.

I had an idea of how I could assist. I would not only have her money when said and done, but I would be able to try some new ideas on her. The tortures I used on Sharon excited me, but because of the collateral disturbances and damages, I couldn't give her the attention she warranted.

Wriley might be different.

Beth Simpson

Beth didn't know what happened to Mike. She left him on her bed to rest after fighting the big man, the one who killed all their friends and her little sister, while she called the Police and EMS. She had to call her parents, too.

When her Mom answered, Beth tried to relay the distressing news as calmly as possible, but the reality that her little sister had probably been killed finally sunk in, and all that came out were sobs.

"Beth, honey?" Katy Simpson could not understand anything her oldest daughter said. "Beth, what's wrong?" She heard in the background a knock followed by some adults talking to Beth. The girl could hardly get a word or two between the racks of weeping. Beth's sorrowful wails faded a bit and a strong male voice came on the line.

"This is Detective Mathis, who is this, please?"

"I'm Katy Simpson, Beth's mother. Detective, what's going on?"

"That's what we're here to find out ma'am." Mathis

spoke as if he had more information than he wanted to share. "There may have been some trouble, Mrs. Simpson, but honestly, we just arrived and haven't gotten any details as yet."

Katy tried to get anything from the man. Bob, her husband, had come to her side, hearing her trying to talk to Beth. He took the phone from her, "This is Bob Simpson. Who am I speaking with?"

"Mr. Simpson, this is Detective Mathis, with the County Sheriff's Office."

"Well, Detective, I suggest you tell me what exactly is going on." Bob had no patience for being jerked around.

"We've only just arrived, Mr. Simpson. All we know is we got a 911 call from this location. Details have not been disclosed yet."

"Okay, Detective," Bob's voice started sounding forced, as if his patience neared its crest, "I suggest you get some answers. Have you tried talking to our youngest daughter?"

"As I said, we've just arrived. The door was open and we found one young lady sobbing uncontrollably on the phone. We haven't seen anyone else. If you give me your number, as soon as we have some information to share, I would be happy to call you back."

Bob hesitated. Only one young lady, no young girl? "We are in Nevada at a conference. We're heading back now." Bob gave him their cell numbers and said they would be there in an hour and a half.

Detective Mathis found Officer Christine Metz with Beth in the family room. Metz proved a valuable asset when dealing with emotional witnesses; her ataractic demeanor seemed to envelop and help relax people in a distraught state. He worked with her on several past cases and when the Sheriff handed him this one, he requested that she be assigned to him.

He motioned her aside. "Find out anything?"

"Her name's Beth. Yesterday she celebrated her 21st, invited some friends over for a party." Metz had been calming Beth as Mathis talked with the parents, coaxing what details she could. "She said she heard a scream from the woods, recognized her sister's voice. There were six people left at the party and they broke into groups of two so they could look for her. That's as far as I got."

They both went back to Beth. Slightly more composed, her uncontrollable sobbing stopped but tears still leaked down her pretty cheeks.

Mathis sat on the table in front of her, while Metz resumed the place next to her on the sofa. He said, "I know this must be difficult, Beth, but we still need some more information. Did you see any of your other friends, or your sister, after everyone split off?"

Beth shook her head and wiped her nose with a tissue. "No. Mike and I took the path that led farther back on the property. We found this car, an old model station wagon, hidden under a big willow tree. The windows were tinted really dark so we couldn't see inside. Then, we heard screams and made our way towards the house.

"We saw this big guy come out of the shack. He carried a machete and had a bloody cloth wrapped around his forearm. He went into the main house and Mike and I followed him.

"We found our way in through a broken out window. Mike said we had to be careful not to make noise. When we got to the base of the stairway, we heard sounds from upstairs. I could hear Becca asking some questions, and a deep voice mumbling replies. Then we heard her scream.

"When we got upstairs, we saw him dragging her out of the room by her ankles, and then the fight between him and Mike started. I got the gun, but he knocked me down, and I hit my head.

"By the time I came to, they were in the room, the big guy shot in the chest and Mike unconscious next to him. Pete was nearby, too, but I could tell he was already dead because his head just... didn't look right, you know?

"I shook Mike awake and we came back here, then I cleaned him up a little before he went to sleep, and I called 911."

A knock on the door interrupted them and an officer came in. Mathis went over to him and said, "Take some officers and start searching the woods out back. We're looking for seven or eight young adults and one juvenile. Keep me posted on progress."

As he left, Mathis sat on the opposite side of Metz, and they tried to get more information. "So, where's Mike now?"

"He should still be upstairs." She led them up, but when she opened the door, Mike had gone. "He's not here," she sounded a little distressed. "I left him here, asleep. Where could he..."

The radio crackled to life calling for Mathis. The voice carried a distressed note, so he excused himself to step out into the hallway.

"Whaddaya got, Jake?"

"Detective, you're going to want to see this." Mathis could hear another officer in the background retching. Not a good sign.

"Where?"

"The old Harris farm."

Mathis walked out the back door after he told Metz to stay and try to get more information from Beth. Before he got to the property line, some hundred yards from Beth's house, he saw a blanket on the ground at the base of a tree, two half-drank beer bottles beside it and a small skirt of white denim material. The tree-edge of the blanket had a darker mark which drew his eyes up the trunk to a jagged stub of a branch. Remains of gore dripped off it.

Mathis had seen some gruesome scenes when he served on a big city force, but he never got used to the atrocities one human could do to another.

A gasp behind him caused him to turn to see Beth standing with her hands covering her mouth, eyes wide at seeing the evidence of foul play. Metz came running up. When she saw it, too, she grasped Beth by the shoulders and turned her away, her own eyes tracking down from the messy stump to the stained blanket.

The glare from Mathis gave her all the reprimand she needed, she narrowed her eyes in return.

He told them, "Well since you're here, you might as well come the rest of the way. Maybe you can show us what you described." With that, he turned and continued to where he had been summoned.

As they broke the tree line, Beth said, "We all split up, Pete and Becca towards that building, Billy and Jill walked down toward the road, and Mike and I went toward the back end." She continued her narration as they all three neared the building that Officer Jake O'Hannesey had called from.

Mathis came around the corner first to see another uniformed officer leaning on the far corner unswallowing whatever he had eaten for breakfast. Another bad omen.

"Metz, you wait with Beth here." He turned to look at both women, his gaze drilling into his subordinate. "You. Two. Wait. Here." The order unmistakable.

Tears welled in Beth's green eyes at the implication, and as soon as she saw Mathis enter, she bolted from the grip that tried to retain her. She got as far as the doorway and froze as Metz caught up and stopped her, but she had already seen the carnage within.

Her little sister lay just inside, her pretty face bruised, bleeding from her mouth, and the wounds from a large knife in her shoulder and her chest. She wore only her pink camisole top and blue panties; at least it didn't look as though the killer tried anything sexual. Her wrists and ankles showed signs of the ligatures that had held her, and the raw, bloody wounds indicated she had not been released, she freed herself.

Beth tried to scream, emitting only a hoarse gurgle, and brought her fists up to her mouth, but would not allow herself to be turned from the grisly scene. Right next to Tammy lay Jill, a large gash across her torso had severed her belly and sternum and her vital organs had spilled out onto the dirt floor.

Further in, she recognized Sharon's headless corpse tied in much the same fashion as Tammy looked like she had been. Her arms had been pulled above her head and her legs slightly spread, rusty metal wire wrapped tightly around her wrists and ankles secured to t-posts driven into the ground.

More time had been spent on Sharon, plus she had screwdrivers in her palms and through the backs of her ankles. The skin on top of her feet, what remained, had been ripped apart, not much meat remaining to cover the scratched bones. Her knees had been smashed to pulp, her breasts severed, cuts and abrasions all over the rest of her body. Her head rested in a corner five feet away, as if it had been tossed aside after being removed.

Metz released her and joined the second officer in redecorating the ground with the contents of her stomach, but Beth kept surveying the scene inside. Mathis seemed unaware she had entered the room.

To the right of Sharon's body, she saw Billy laying holding his leg, a large gash on his upper thigh. The large, congealed puddle of blood around him bespoke his slow death.

Mathis had his back to the front of the room where she stood, discussing the probable events that had taken place with O'Hannesey. When he stepped to the side, the officer saw the girl and motioned toward her.

Mathis looked and saw her glancing around the room, taking it all in. He closed his eyes and hung his head, slowly moving it side to side. No sign of Metz. He began walking toward Beth, but not before she saw the final body in the room.

Jer lay sprawled lazily against the wall, half his face obliterated by the branch and his eye dangling against his cheek. Beth continued to scan over the grisly sight as Mathis approached and put a hand on her shoulder.

"I told you to stay back." His voice soft, he offered what platitudes he could. Copious tears flowed down her cheeks. Any makeup she might have worn the night before had been washed away by then.

He shot Metz an angry look when she reappeared, but Beth spoke up, "I had to see, Detective. This is my little sister, my friends. I had to know." The pain in her eyes softened his ire.

He decided this young woman had more strength than he gave her credit for. She had surveyed the bodies with more aplomb than several of his officers, Metz included. When he asked if all the people were accounted for, she told him again of the last two and the killer inside the house and turned to lead them.

Metz started to restrain her, but Mathis waved her off. They followed Beth up to the main house. Inside, she picked her way around the rotten areas and ascended the stairs, pointing out the trouble spots as they went.

On the landing, she recounted the events, indicating where Becca's body still rested, where Mike and the killer stood, and where she crept up behind them when she got ahold of the pistol.

She couldn't say how the final moments went after

she had her feet kicked from under her and knocked her head on the floor. A circular dent showed where her head had hit the softened, rotting boards.

They all went into the room and saw Pete exactly where she told them. The killer sprawled not far from him, a gaping wound in his gut and a large puddle of blood around him. There were footprints near the body, which Beth informed Mathis were from when Mike had taken the keys off the killer.

Outside, they heard the arrival of the first ambulance, sirens winding down as the tires skidded on the dirt. Mathis directed everyone out. "We need to get some more transports, and see if the Coroner has made it yet." He heaved a sigh, looking over the scene again, and mumbled, "This is going to be a long day."

When he finished assigning Officers to certain areas to log the gruesome scenes, Mathis took Beth back to her house. No sooner had they walked in when her parents burst in the door.

Her mother pulled Beth close for a tight hug while Bob approached Mathis. "Have you found Tammy, Detective?" The distress in his voice caused Mathis to motion a couple of officers in from the front yard that had been watching.

"Mr. Simpson, please." He waved his hand toward the couch, hoping to try to break the news gently. There were not many ways to tell a parent that one of his children had been killed. Bob refused to move and became more distraught when he didn't get immediate confirmation that his baby girl was safe.

He saw the back door open and tried to force his way past Mathis only to be caught by both arms. "Get off me!" His voice becoming more enraged when he couldn't search for her himself. "Where's Tammy? Tammy!"

An ambulance crew had arrived, and Mathis waved

them over. One put down his case and began preparing a syringe with a sedative as the other helped hold the man still. The needle jabbed home and the liquid surged into his arm. As he calmed down, the cops led him to sit on the sofa with his wife and eldest daughter. They both moved away to accept him between them and embraced his sobbing form.

Mathis hated that part of the job. Usually, the mother had to be sedated, but it seemed the females of the Simpson family had a bit more resilience than most. In as gentle a way as possible, he relayed the facts that had been presented and shown to him. The mother didn't make it far before she had begun crying as well, but she didn't become hysterical enough to need sedation.

When the news had been told, Mathis relayed his sympathies and excused himself, telling the Officers and EMS to stay close in case they were needed. He went back out to return to the farm.

Katy tried to ask Beth if she had been hurt, but Bob started accusing her of being to blame. "If you hadn't thrown a party... If you had made sure she went to Julie's house..."

Coming to her eldest daughter's defense, Katy said, "Bob, stop. This isn't Beth's fault. How dare you try to blame her?"

The hurt in his girl's eyes brought him to his senses. Like a chastised child, he hung his head and mumbled, "I'm sorry."

"Daddy, believe me, had I known..."

"I know, Baby. No one could have known. I just wish we hadn't gone to that damned convention."

"We didn't know, either, Bob. Stop it, now. None of us are to blame."

Beth needed to be alone. She excused herself and went back to her room. On the nightstand, she saw the envelope Mike showed her; the one he and Jer found in

Sharon's purse. She closed the door and went over to look inside. She estimated it held over twenty thousand dollars, and wondered why he would have left it. Unless he had access to more that she didn't know about. Sharon was, after all, a conniving bitch.

Wriley Canton

Wriley Canton had been, as the saying goes, born with a silver spoon in her mouth. Her parents tried to keep her from being a spoiled brat, but as she had golden curls on her head, almost clear blue eyes, and a constant dimple in her right cheek, her adorable looks let her get away with more than the average child would.

For many years, she had been able to convince her parents' friends, especially the men, to get her little things without getting caught, but those days had dwindled as she aged. She found herself hard pressed to find someone gullible enough to keep falling for her charms. It didn't help that her body had developed, earlier and more than most other girls. Most of the men started shying away from her after puberty set in, probably afraid they would be accused of indiscretions were they to be alone with her.

When she came of age, she had to start doing naughty things to get some of the men to comply. When that became necessary, she demanded cash instead of things. She had no intention of being a prostitute, but she could get money just by doing those little favors. She never actually had sex with them.

In her twenties, she went away to a university. Based on all the college movies she had seen, she thought it an opportunity to party. She didn't realize until too late that she would be expected to do some actual work. She dropped out after a year, with less than positive marks.

Her parents were a bit disgruntled by her choices and actions. They just could not understand how she acquired the inclinations she had. They would cease talking when she came into the room, walk around her as if they feared to touch her, and respond to her questions in clipped mutterings. It took a year for them to get through the anger and confusion, compounded frequently with her continued misadventures.

Then, they died. She thought it so cliché and found herself more flustered than before. She based her decision to go to college on the movies she'd seen and had been disappointed. She realized that movies don't mirror real life. Then her parents got killed in a fashion overused by movie makers.

They were driving home from a gathering late at night. Somehow, her dad lost control while negotiating the curvy, hilly roadway, and the car flew off the road. When they hit the bottom, after a fifty-foot drop, the car exploded. The investigators could not verify if they had been killed before the landing or not.

Wriley sank into a mental abyss. She didn't respond to any stimuli and needed constant assistance 24 hours a day. Doctors would visit to administer care, and psychiatrists would try to pull her from her funk. Then, with no warning, she snapped out of it.

Her inheritance had specific rules, governed by her father's will. She would be given a stipend every week, and when she could not make it last, the payments switched to a daily amount. No longer able to sway any of her father's male friends, her allowance became her sole income.

She needed to figure out how to get her hands on more of her cash so she would be able to get some trendy items to keep up with her friends. Try as she might, though, she just could not get around the security provisions set forth. She felt embarrassed about being in her thirties and not being able to use whatever money she wanted when she wanted.

One Sunday night, she pulled into Danse Club, her usual haunt, and drove to the back of the lot to park. She found an empty spot next to a sturdy looking classic 4-wheel-drive car. She called every motor vehicle a "car."

Inside, she sought her party friends, plopping into the round booth as one of the guys slid over. Loud greetings mixed with their laughter as they enveloped her into the conversation already in progress.

Wriley began, once again, to bemoan her situation; that she could only get a set amount of cash no matter how she tried to manipulate them to let her have more.

Her friends quieted, eyes going wide and looking behind and above her. When she turned, she saw a man standing right beside her. Her gaze traveled up but she couldn't see his face, as he stood under a bright spotlight.

"I might be able to help," he said just loud enough for her to hear above the pounding electronic beats emanating from the speakers all around the room.

He drew her aside so they could speak privately, while her friends discussed possible rumors to throw around. She shared her dilemma with willing abandon, desperate to get her hands on more cash regardless the means.

"I'll do anything to get my money," she told him. "Anything." She emphasized the word while looking directly at him, then let her gaze roam towards his groin to further make her meaning clear.

"We'll see about that," he said. "Give me the details."

She relayed how her net worth landed somewhere in the millions, though she didn't know the exact amount. Her father never trusted banks, so he kept everything in a safe in the basement and had three people taking care of the disbursements, and had bequeathed enough to them in his will to ensure their continued loyalty even after his demise.

There were also security guards who watched out for them and the property. She had gathered information on their patrol schedules, which she laid out between them, and where they were usually stationed.

"Daddy never trusted too many people; he always had a degree of paranoia.

"Every morning, the accountants go down to the lower levels together. When they come back up, they give me my daily allowance and go about their other duties. I try and try to follow them but never can make it to the safe. The guards and security doors stop me so I can't give any information on what type of safe it is or how to open it."

After she finished, he told her he might have some ideas, but would have to consider them before committing to anything. They made plans to meet the following night and he stood to leave.

"Wait, I don't even know your name." She placed her hand on his, still trying to see his features. He somehow always found a way to keep his face in the shadows, thus making it difficult to see any real details about his description.

He turned but hesitated a moment. "Mike," he told her, then made his way out the door. When she tried to follow, a group of people flooded through the entrance. By the time she got outside, he had gone, as had the classic car she parked next to.

The next night, she waited at the same table they had

used, watching the door for him to enter. After half an hour, she had just about given up when his hand landed on her shoulder.

"Going somewhere?" He walked around her, pulled the empty chair closer and sat.

She had repositioned the chairs so his face would be more in the light, but he maneuvered it just right to foil her scheme.

She tried to glean some personal information from him, and he avoided all but the most uninformative details. He had every intention to help get her money, so she let his desire for privacy prevail.

For two more hours, they discussed her situation. She felt some of his questions didn't address the subject, and wanted to confront him about it. However, the thoughts flew from her mind while they talked, as he seemed most adept at squashing any doubts.

"I have it worked out now," he told her as he upended his glass, draining the dregs. "I can follow you to the house tonight. You get me in and find a place for me to hide. In the morning, I'll get your money out of the safe."

Surprised at the sudden revelation, she found it hard to think of all she wanted to ask. "Already? I didn't expect it so soon."

"You seemed in a hurry. Would you rather forget it?" He leaned in closer to her. The light finally showed his entire face. His eyebrows lowered, and his eyes agitated her stomach

"No," she replied, scared not only of the emptiness she saw, but also a fear of losing what she didn't have yet. "Please, if you know how, tell me."

"I have to be in the house overnight. I'll find the way to the vault and bring the cash to your room. Just remember, once this is set in motion, there's no going back."

The ominous statement caught her off guard. "Even if I have to leave town after, I don't care. I just want the cash."

"Let's get to it, then." He stood and waved his hand in front of him, indicating she should lead the way. "You leave first and wait for me across the road from your driveway."

"I thought you were going to follow me?" She tried to figure out what he had in mind.

"We cannot be seen leaving together. As far as anyone's concerned, we just meet here for drinks and talk." He grabbed her shoulder when she stood. "You haven't told anyone what we've talked about, have you?" The tone of his deep voice, somehow different than how he normally talked, stopped her in her tracks.

"No, of course not." The quaver in her response surprised her. She hadn't told anyone, but his question had her thinking of all discussions she had since they began talking to make sure. "I haven't, I swear. They probably all think I'm trying to get you to fuck me, like I always do."

He smirked, "Is that what you want?" He drew closer to her ear, his deep-voiced whisper sending chills down her spine. She could not tell if the chills were of desire, of fear, or both. "A good, hard fuck?"

"No," she lied. Bowing her head, she immediately admitted, "Yes." She raised her chin and shook her head, her blond curls bouncing with the move as she looked directly at him. "I don't know. You kind of scare me."

He let go of her, his countenance shifting into more of a sneer. "Good. You will be less likely to change your mind that way." He glanced at her body, sending more shivers through her. "And you just might get fucked for your efforts."

Before she could decide if that amounted to an offer or a threat, he changed his demeanor, sending the thought away in an instant.

"Go on now. Wait where the cameras won't see you. I'll be there in less than an hour and we can get the first stage ready."

She found it hard to contain her excitement, but he had warned her not to let her emotions betray them. When she went out, she blindly walked toward where she had parked, looking down into her purse to dig for her keys. She pulled them out and looked back up as she approached her car, which she had again parked next to the old 4X4.

A girl leaned on the bumper of the other car. Small and pretty, with long black hair and green eyes. She wore snug blue jeans, and Wriley had a flash of jealousy of the young lady's petite figure.

"Excuse me," the girl said, "do you know who drives this truck?"

Wriley deliberately didn't look at either the vehicle or the speaker again. She tried jabbing her key in the lock of her door. "Um, no. Sorry," she lied. She felt a tiny hand on her shoulder and turned, about to lash out, but saw a sadness in the girl's eyes. "I said I didn't know."

"I heard, I just wanted to ask: Have you seen this guy in there?" A picture of Mike, but with gorgeous brown eyes instead of black. "My name's Beth. This is a friend of mine and I think he may be in trouble."

"No, he doesn't look familiar. I'm sorry, I have to go." Without looking at Beth again, she dropped into her car and started it up. As she pulled away, she saw Beth in the mirror watching as she drove off.

Beth and Jason

Beth decided she needed to find Mike. There had to be some reason he would simply disappear, plus she could not discount the sense of foreboding in the back of her mind.

Knowing her parents would not understand, she sat and penned a note to them to explain. They would want to know why, with Tammy and several of her close friends murdered so recently, she wouldn't wait until after the funerals to leave.

Dear Mom & Dad,

I know you won't understand but I have to go after Mike. I can't really explain why, it's just a feeling I have that something's not right with him. Somehow, I know that if I don't find him, many more people will be hurt. I will call to let you know I'm okay.

I love you both,

Beth

Gathering together several changes of clothes, she stuffed them into her backpack as neatly as possible. She knew the more time she waited, the more likely one of her parents would happen to be awake and stop her from going.

Since she had the envelope Mike left, she wouldn't have to worry about trying to come up with any money; she could pay for whatever she might need and not even put a dent in the stack of bills courtesy of Sharon.

In the middle of the night, she snuck out the front door and tossed her bag into the back seat of her ten-year-old sedan. She gave thought to trying to push the thing far enough away from the house to start it without risking waking her folks. However, she heard the paramedics say they were leaving some pills in case anyone had trouble sleeping and knew her father would probably need them.

The thought of never seeing her little sister again almost caused her to break down into another crying fit, one which would hinder her ability to operate the vehicle safely. She pushed it aside with the determination to catch up with Mike.

She would be hard pressed to explain, but she felt that she needed to at least try and stop him before someone else got hurt.

Steeling her nerves, she started the car and backed out of the driveway, not even glancing at the house to see if any lights came on.

She drove south, not knowing why outside of the hunch that he went that way. She gave in to following her gut feelings, hoping they proved correct, as she had no other options for finding him.

Crossing the State line into Arizona, she kept driving until she felt she needed to head west. That route took her through a State Park where she could marvel at the changing landscape. The multi-colored hills with their scrub brush alternated with spotted areas of pines were fascinating. She almost wanted to find a place where she could camp out, maybe near a waterfall, but the need to find Mike outweighed everything else.

As she passed some large properties, a station wagon with dark tinted windows pulled onto the road from a driveway lined with a wooden fence painted bright white. She swore it looked like the one she and Mike had discovered at the Harris farm.

She followed it to a small diner and saw an older man get out. On a whim, she parked and went inside.

"Excuse me, sir," she said as she neared the booth he sat in. "I can't help but think your car looks familiar. A friend of mine had one just like it, and I'm looking for him."

He began telling her, with a bit of pride, about the negotiation with the young man who had driven it into his yard, and the deal he had made with the young "feller."

She produced a picture she had of Mike, and the man said, "Well, that looks a lot like him, but the eyes were different."

"How do you mean, 'different'?"

"Darker, perhaps. Ain't seen anyone with eyes like his."

The man continued telling of the discussion they'd had and about the 4-wheel-drive he traded to get it, as well as the direction Mike took when leaving.

Beth had the confirmation that she'd followed the right path and thanked the man, even paying for his meal to show her gratitude. She hopped back into her car and continued the search.

She passed a smaller highway that headed northwest just after she entered Nevada. She felt almost lost after going past it, and on another impulse, made a U-turn to go back. As she approached the intersection, she felt an ease in her anxiety, so she turned to follow that road. When she spotted a small town ahead of her, she noticed a motel on the fringes. She started getting drowsy and figured she should stop for a while.

The old man running the place told her they didn't take credit cards, so she laid her wallet on the counter while counting out the payment. He saw Mike's photo and let out a "Huh."

She looked at him, "What...?" Following his gaze, she pulled up the picture. "You've seen this man?"

"Funny. Tha's the last guy stopped in. Couple days ago. Seemed nice 'nuff, but sumpin's kinda off with 'im."

"'Off,' how?"

"Cain't tell, really, jus'..." He trailed off, then turned and got her linens and told her about letting the customers take care of making the beds to keep prices down. Beth thanked him as she took the towels and sheets. "Ya want the same room he had?"

Not even having considered that option, she decided it might be beneficial somehow. "Why, sure. Thank you." The idea to leave her car in front of the office flitted across her mind, only to be quashed when she lowered herself into the driver's seat.

Inside the room, she went about preparing to get some rest. She pulled off her soiled clothes and slipped on the negligee she usually slept in, then dressed the bed and slipped in. Sleep found her quickly.

In her dreams, Mike found a woman with much the same build as Sharon. There were piles of money covered in blood, a large blade dripping with gore raised and swung down. The last thing she remembered from it was a long, shrill scream, and she sat bolt upright, the bed and sheets soaking wet with her sweat.

She hung her legs over the edge of the bed and cradled her head, then ran her fingers through her long black hair, trying to make sense of the dream. Standing, she went into the bathroom and turned on the hot water in the shower.

When she looked in the mirror, she saw the woman

standing behind her. The face covered in cuts and neck slashed, the image reached for Beth with gaping gashes on her arms and huge, bloody wounds on her chest, mouthing "Help."

Beth brought her hands to her mouth. Suppressing a scream, she turned to find nothing there. Breathing hard, Beth leaned on the sink to gather her wits, then finished her duties. After she dressed, she scanned the room to make sure she didn't forget anything.

She had to get back on the road. She had to find Mike before he did something to someone else.

That thought made her stop before she got to the door. Why would she think "someone else?" Mike hadn't done anything as far as she knew, but somehow, she knew he had taken up where the killer they stopped had left off. Maybe, she thought, some kind of thing had been responsible, not the actual person doing the killing?

That made no sense. She shook it off and got back on the road after returning the key.

When she saw the first highway past the California border, she turned south again. She hadn't even been paying much attention as her mind still dwelt on the dream, the woman with the cut-up face and body.

Passing through some mountainous terrain, she only half saw the scenery, the nice houses on large properties. She passed a group of buildings, some apartments and houses mixed in with small businesses. Just after those, she saw a large casino labeled "Cody Bill's," and set off behind everything else stood another sign with "Danse Club" flashing in multicolored neon.

Feeling a pull toward it, she turned in and drove to the back of the property. The lot had quite a few vehicles for a Monday, but as the gambling place played the centerpiece, maybe large crowds were the norm no matter the day of the week.

Continuing around to the back side, she caught her

breath. The 4×4 described by the old gentleman sat in one of the spaces. She looked for a spot of her own but had to circle the place again. The first one she found, after weaving through several of the outer lanes, she pulled into.

She went back to the truck and leaned her backside on the back bumper, hoping Mike would come out so she could confront him.

Soon, she saw a lady approaching, bearing a striking resemblance to the one she saw in her dream, fumbling in her purse for keys as she walked to the car next to the 4X4. Beth pulled out Mike's picture and asked, "Excuse me, do you know who drives this truck?"

The lady hardly looked at her, hands shaking as she tried several times to get the key into the lock. "Um, no, sorry."

Beth placed her hand on the lady's shoulder, wanting to ask if she felt okay. Maybe she had drunk too much and needed help.

The woman turned about, a storm brewing in her blue eyes, but softened when she looked at Beth. "I said I didn't know."

Beth introduced herself and showed Mike's photo, but the lady hardly looked at it. Denying knowledge again, she turned and slunk into her car, started it, and backed out. Beth could only watch as she drove away.

She walked toward the club, went in and paid the entry fee, then made her way through the mob toward the bar. When the bartender finally made it to her, she pulled the picture out.

"Have you seen this man?" She practically had to scream over the thumping electronic beats issuing from the multitude of speakers.

The lady, fairly attractive and around her mother's age, glanced at it and shook her head. Before she turned, she stopped and took it to look closer. "Yeah, I have," she said, leaning over to get closer. Her breath smelled a little of whiskey and beer. "I think he just left."

Beth thanked her and turned to leave, but the bartender grabbed her wrist and pointed to a sign, "Two Drink Minimum," so she ordered two shots and two beers. When they came, she laid a twenty down and pushed them back at her saying, "Enjoy!" as she walked out.

She hadn't seen Mike leave, as she had been paying more attention to weaving through the crowd, but when she got back outside the truck was gone. She heaved a sigh and decided to find a place for the night, intending to try again the next day.

As the thumping of the music from inside dwindled, she heard someone running toward her. A man's voice hailed her, "Hey, wait a minute." She turned, fully expecting to defend her two-drink choice. "I heard you asking Janet if she saw someone. Could I see the picture?"

The man dressed well, wearing a light blue button-down shirt and a loosened dark blue tie with gray slacks. His short blond hair parted on the left and he kept his face clean-shaven. His nose seemed a bit large, but his long jawline gave him an attractive visage.

She reached into her purse and pulled out her wallet, excitement making her hands shake a little as she produced the photo again. He looked at it, nodding his head. "Yeah, that's him."

"You have seen him?"

"Yeah, he's been talking to my friend, Wriley. She's been trying to figure out how to get her hands on more of her money, but her parents left strict provisions when they died last year."

Beth looked around, trying to find a better place to talk, but everything around looked made to make noise. She yawned, though she tried to hide it. "Look, I'd really like to find out more. Is there someplace a little less noisy we could go?"

He shook his head. "You look like you need to rest. Have you been on the road long?"

She nodded. "All day, actually. Yesterday, too."

"Okay. You see over across the highway, there?" He pointed to a housing area, and she nodded again. He pulled a card from his wallet, wrote on the back, and handed it to her. "Go find this place, tell her Jason Makeland sent you, and she'll set you up with a bed to crash on."

She read the card, "Cody's B&B, For After A Night Of Fun." Her eyes narrowed when she looked back at Jason. "Are you setting me up?"

He smiled affably, shaking his head. "No, I'm trying to help you, and my friend. You go there, she'll get you sorted out. It will still cost, but not the bloated price for the regular clients. I'll stop by around 8 in the morning, then we can go have breakfast and talk."

She relaxed and agreed. When he walked away, he didn't turn to look back at her. She got into her car and went to find the Bed and Breakfast.

The place turned out not being too hard to find. She knocked on the front door. A moment later, an elderly lady opened. "May I help you?" Her voice shook a little from age and she looked like she had been beautiful in her younger years. Even though she had to be in her sixties, maybe older, she still had a very attractive appearance. She had a pleasing smile and her silvery, bob-cut hair accentuated her round face.

Beth handed her the card. "Jason Makeland told me to come see about a place to sleep."

The lady's face brightened. "Such a sweet boy. Of course, come on in." She pulled the door wide and ushered Beth into the parlor. "Now, I do have a couple of beds open. Since Jason recommended you, I can offer you a discounted price. Half of what others pay. Would that be alright?" She had an easy way about her, and even the doubled price usually charged would seem like a bargain coming from her.

Beth smiled, relaxing. She half expected to be run over the coals or taken for a lot of money. "That's fine," she said. "Thank you."

The woman introduced herself as Edith as she recited the rules of the house. None of them sounded much different than the guidelines Beth had been raised with.

With the transaction completed, Edith showed her upstairs to a room at the end of the hall. "I don't have many guests tonight, so nobody is in the room next to it. Should be nice and quiet for you. The bath adjoins the two rooms, but like I said, no one is in there, so you'll have it to yourself."

When she handed Beth the key, she turned and shuffled back down the stairs. On the third step, she turned, "Will you be joining us for breakfast as well?"

"I'm not sure, Edith. Jason said he'd come by at 8. We have something to discuss, about a friend of mine that I'm looking for, so we'll need a bit of privacy."

Edith bobbed her head in understanding as she resumed her trek downstairs.

Beth went into her room. The double bed had a white comforter with pink flowery designs. The nightstand, stained dark, held a faux crystal lamp with a white shade. It also had a dresser with three drawers and a television on top.

She set her small bag and her purse on the metal support at the end of the bed and pulled out her sleeping garment, a pink camisole top and loose shorts. When she went into the bathroom to clean up and change for bed, she admired the towels and rug that matched the cover on the bed.

She tried the door leading to the next room and found

it only opened from the other side. Looking back at the door to her room, she saw the same thing. No one could open the wrong door. She wondered if something prevented both from being open at the same time.

She showered and dressed, then slid into the big, comfy bed and fell asleep in record time. In her dreams, she saw Mike stumbling down a rocky slope. Rain fell hard, making the descent slippery, but he got to a shelf just wide enough to walk on that hid him from the warehouses above.

Several men looked down, standing beside a car wrecked at a guardrail, with their guns drawn. She couldn't tell how many people were searching for him. Some of them had pistols while others held small semi-automatic rifles she thought might be Uzis. Larger than the pistols but smaller than the rifles she'd seen men carrying for hunting back home.

Mike edged his way along the cliff staying just out of sight of those above until he came to a slight alcove where he had to stop. To continue would have revealed his exact position. He hunkered down as the men up top began fanning out and throwing stones down trying to get him to reveal his position. Mike raised and shot, hitting one guard and causing him to roll down the hill. As he did, others saw him, and their shots rang out.

Mike took a bullet to the shoulder that spun him around and caused him to lose his footing and tumble over the ledge. Beth woke with a scream in her throat, a loud knocking on the door.

The sun had cleared the horizon and the room stood bright in her eyes, clogged with drying tears. The knocking sounded again, and she rolled out of the bed, oblivious to her state of dress, and opened the door.

Jason stood there with a concerned look. He wore a beige shirt, the top two buttons undone, over a pair of dark brown slacks.

The look in her eyes caused him to furrow his brow. Like she didn't fully realize where she was. He noticed she didn't have much on and pushed his way in, backing her to the bed as he pulled the sheet off and around her, then had her sit down beside him.

"Beth." He spoke soft, trying to ease her out of whatever dream she might still be lost in. "Beth, are you with me?"

She looked up and scanned the room as if trying to get her bearings. Jason went into the bathroom, got a washcloth and wet it in the sink. Returning to her, he resumed

"Beth, come on." He lay his hand on the side of her pretty face and gently patted her cheek to bring her out of her fog.

Her gaze fell on him. Her mouth turned down as she narrowed her eyes and tried to push away. He held her, his arm around her shoulders until she calmed down, still speaking her name in a gentle voice.

"Jason? What are you doing here?" She still seemed a bit disoriented, looking around the room.

He smiled. "I came to get you for breakfast. I got to your door and heard you scream out." He kept his voice soft. "Are you okay?"

She looked down, noticing the sheet around her and her vision shot back to him. She blushed a bit, realizing she still wore her nighties and must have opened the door for him in them. Seeing her embarrassment, he put on a half-smile and said, "It's alright, I didn't look."

He helped her up, still holding the sheet around her, and led her to the bathroom. "Get a shower. I'll wait for you downstairs." He went to the door and looked back, seeing her still just standing there. "Beth." She looked at him and he pointed into the chamber. "Shower, dress. We don't have a lot of time, I think." He went out as she shuffled through the door.

Half an hour later, she came down wearing her blue jeans and a blue tee shirt with an image of wolves on the front.

"Feel any better?" He still had some concern in his voice. He placed the cup of coffee he had been sipping on the small table next to him.

"Yeah, a little." She kept her eyes downward, not wanting to look directly at him.

He stood and approached her, but kept his hands in his pockets, trying not to spook her more. "Beth, it's okay. It's nothing I haven't seen my little sister wearing." He ducked down trying to catch her eyes. "Besides, you kind of remind me of her."

She glanced at him and saw his playful smirk. "I just," she stammered. "I'm sorry." Finally looking at him, she realized he meant well and didn't want her to be ashamed. She looked away again, trying to remember the dream that eluded her. "I'm not sure what happened. Some dream I can't remember, and all the sudden you were there, and I still had on my night clothes. I thought," she looked back at him.

"It doesn't matter. You didn't do anything wrong." He smiled again. "Neither did I." She smiled, too. "Good. Like I said, I don't think we have much time. You ready to go?"

She raised her bag, "All packed up."

Edith came in asking if they would join her. Jason approached, taking her hands. "We can't, Grandma."

Beth realized, *'She is his grandma, no wonder he could recommend someone and they'd get a discount.'*

He continued, nodding in Beth's direction, "We need to talk in private. I'll tell you all about it later, okay?"

Edith looked at Beth, concern clouding her lovely blue eyes. "Didn't you sleep well, Dear?"

Beth didn't want her to worry. The lady reminded her of her own Grandma. "I'm okay. Just a little nightmare."

"I'll explain later, Gramma. We need to go." He kissed her cheek and led Beth out the door.

He took her to a little diner not far away. When they went in, she noticed there didn't seem to be many customers. He walked toward a booth in the back and slid in, motioning to the other side. As Beth lowered herself onto the thick red vinyl, the waitress appeared behind her with a couple of coffee cups and the urn. She filled the cups and looked at Jason with eyebrows raised.

"Oh. Becky, this is Beth. Beth, Becky." He had another of his winning smiles as the girls shook hands.

"Hi, Beth." Becky had a nice smile. She looked to be in her thirties, with her blond hair pulled back slack enough to cover her ears and bound in a ponytail that reached her waist. Slim, but not to the point of being skinny, and about three inches taller than Beth. Her uniform came down to her knees showing off firm, tanned calves down to her bright pink tennis shoes. "Breakfast?"

Beth noticed the concern tinting her look and nodded, picking up a menu to divert the attention. "Let me look for a minute?"

Becky bobbed her head, looking back at Jason with the unspoken question. "Give us a couple of minutes, 'kay?"

The woman moved off. Beth lay the menu in front of her and leaned over toward him. "Do I look that bad?"

He almost danced around the answer, but she cocked her head. "A little harried, maybe." She glanced around, using her left hand to move some hair behind her ear. Jason placed his hand on hers. "Hey, don't worry. Do you know how many people come in here the day after they lose everything at the casino? They look much worse than you ever could."

When she looked up, she expected to see sarcasm, but didn't. He backed off to give her time to decide on a meal.

While they ate, he made small talk, asking about her history. He seemed saddened when he learned her sister had been killed. When she told him about the confrontation with the killer, he just sat with his chin in his rounded fingers, looking off to the side. Then she got to the disappearance of Mike.

"I don't know, but I think somehow, Mike took up where that guy left off." She expected him to laugh, but he just sat there. "Don't you think that's weird?"

He straightened his back as Becky came and refilled their coffee. He smiled at the lady and told her they would be done in a minute. The restaurant had filled up in the time they sat, but the waitress had put some store-related items on the only table nearby so they could talk in private. Nothing had been said to indicate they needed it, she just seemed to know.

He leaned back, one eyebrow raised as he thrummed his fingers on the table. She felt sure he would walk away, or send her off, scorning her tale. "Let me tell you something," he started.

Oh, boy, here it comes, she thought.

"I do believe you." She looked at him, thinking again he meant to ridicule her. "I knew a girl. Her name was Allie."

"'Was?'"

"Yeah, she died not long ago, too. Killed, more accurately." He leaned toward her, his elbows on the table. "I lived up in Idaho. My company opened a branch there and I had to oversee the operations for a while, so she went with me.

"She looked a lot like you, in fact. But before she disappeared," he looked over her shoulder to make sure no one listened in, "she started changing. She became distant. Not morose really, but like she wanted to find something. I tried to talk to her, to find out what." He looked off, his eyes watering over.

"You loved her, didn't you?"

He glanced back and smiled. "Of course I did." His voice caught a little. "She was my little sister."

That surprised Beth. "So, what does this have to do with Mike?"

"When the Police found her, a car had been left and hers was gone. They traced the registration to a guy named Joel. Joel Jones." He reached into his back pocket and pulled out a picture. It looked exactly like the big guy that killed her friends.

Beth looked at Jason. "I don't understand."

"Allie got into some weird shit," he told her. "Some kind of Occult stuff maybe, but I'm not sure. A group of people she started hanging out with, I think, filled her head with a bunch of demon lore or some bullshit.

"I noticed her attitude changed, she didn't act like herself. I didn't know for sure what happened, nor what to do about it.

"Then, she disappeared. I tracked her by her phone and found her dead." He lowered his voice more and whispered, "He had punched her in the face, at least twice. He beat her to death." Beth could hear the quaver in his voice. "The cops wrote it off, especially after finding out about the crowd she had been hanging around. But I had a feeling, like a pull that I had to follow. It led me back here."

"Back?" Beth still tried to tie everything together in her head.

"We grew up here." He looked around again. "The casino is the family business."

Her eyes went wide. She looked down, glancing side to side but not looking at anything.

"The girl you spoke with last night, Wriley? I've known her all our lives. She's never been satisfied with what she had. She would do anything to get more. Just like Sharon."

Beth snapped her sight back to him. How did he know about her?

"I told you, I have a sense about this thing. It's like a part of Allie is still there. And she's calling out for me to help. Then, there are the dreams."

She wanted to scoff, but what he said didn't sound any more outlandish than what she felt. "I kind of feel that about Mike. Like he's drawing me to follow. Asking me to help him somehow." Her brow crinkled, and a tear fell from her green eyes.

"I know, Beth. I can feel all three of them calling me. Like they're appalled at the actions, but have no control."

"So, what do we do?"

"I think it's too late to save Wriley. I know we can't save Mike, but maybe we can keep this thing from going any further.

"By the way, can you tell me anything about your dreams? It's important."

Beth told him she had seen Wriley. "She had cuts all over her face. She reached for me, asking for help. Then the dream changed, and I saw someone chasing Mike through some warehouses both on foot and by vehicle, through a heavy downpour. He wrecked, then went downhill to a ledge. The men chasing him didn't follow, but stood watch above."

"That sounds like it's near the places Wriley's father used to run. A bunch of warehouses he rented out to different companies. They all closed down about ten years ago, just after he died."

"There's more," Beth said. "After he made it down, he got shot and fell off."

"That might not be the best way to kill him."

"What's that mean?" She looked almost angry at the mention of him dying.

Jason rubbed the back of his neck as he looked out into the parking lot. Heaving a sigh, he looked back at her. "Look, Beth. You have to realize there may be no way to keep Mike from getting killed."

She turned her head away to hide the tears that threatened to overflow.

He continued, "We might be able to make sure he gets killed *right*."

She shot her gaze back to him. "How can you be so callous? What, are you just pissed your sister died, now you want anyone else involved in any way to die, too?" The tears had escaped their confines and flowed free down her cheeks.

"Beth," his voice had gone soft again, a tremor announcing his grief. "I don't want anyone else to die. You must accept that there is a very real possibility that he will. The guards at Wriley's place? They don't get to do much. If they find her dead, killed by an intruder, they will use everything they have to make sure the person responsible doesn't get off the property."

She nodded and grabbed some napkins to dry her eyes and face. "So, what do you mean by the best way?"

He told her about when he had the same kinds of dreams about Allie. He tracked down one of the girls in the group she had been involved with and pressed to get some information from her. They had somehow released an entity through their "experiments," as they called them.

He couldn't get all the particulars, but they figured that it would be able to transfer from one host to another by way of murder. The carrier would have to be killed, most likely in a violent manner, and it would be released and invade the one who did it. That's how Mike ended up with it. Though not legally classed as murder, the death of Joel came about brutally, and Mike did the deed.

"I figure somehow, the people who had been closest

to the host can sense what's going on. Like the person might be reaching out for help. But so far, we haven't been able to get there in time."

"So, you're saying that Mike is sending me some kind of psychic plea for help?" She had some doubts about that, but in the back of her mind, she felt it might be true.

"I'm not sure, Beth."

She checked her watch then looked outside. Dark clouds had rolled in, thunder rumbling in the distance. "Shit, we need to go. The dream had heavy rains, and it looks like it's about to start."

Jason paid the bill and they got in their separate cars. He led her to the Canton Estate. As they got close, the rain started pouring down. No sprinkle to announce it, just a sudden downpour.

The Mansion

Wriley couldn't get that girl Beth out of her mind. Something in her green eyes hinted concern, loneliness, a sadness that went much deeper than a missing friend.

As she drove the winding road that led to her front gate, she thought about some of the ways Mike might be able to get her money. That's all she really wanted, to finally get her hands on all the cash. She shouldn't have a restriction on how much she could spend. It's her money, damn it, she should be able to do whatever she wanted with it, whenever she wanted.

She pulled to the shoulder to wait. Mike told her he would be along in a few minutes. They would hide him in the back of her car so she could get him onto the property, then go to her parking garage on the back side of the building. Her daddy made that one just for her when she first started driving. He didn't trust her parking with all the fancy old cars he liked to collect.

When they got inside, he would wait while she checked the hallways to her staircase, then take him up to her rooms and find him a place to sleep. In the morning, he would find a way around the guards to the basement, where the safe had been built and wait for the CPA guy to open it somewhere around 10.

She didn't want to know how he meant to get in or out from that point, and she didn't really care. She wouldn't even worry if he got caught, she could deny knowledge of his plan. Claim ignorance. Her word against his, if he tried to involve her. Maybe he climbed into her trunk while she spent time with her friends at Danse Club, she could say.

Brought out of her thoughts by a pair of headlights coming around the curve behind her, Wriley got out and leaned on the side of her car. No one ever used this road except those coming and going from her house, unless they had gotten lost; it went past her driveway for about a mile, then ended at a big chain link gate leading to her dad's old warehouse area. That place had closed a decade ago and no one went there anymore.

The old blue and white 4X4 pulled up behind her. She just knew he drove that car. He got out and walked over to her and said, "Is there somewhere to park this where no one will see it? We don't want to alert anyone by having a vehicle sitting empty on the side of the road."

"Only if you drive it over a hill," she told him, pointing across the road.

"Wriley, it's a four-wheel drive. It's made to drive over much more than just a hill." His smile looked almost condescending, but she let it slide. She didn't care what it had been made for; if he got it stuck he wouldn't be able to get away when they were done with their plans.

He reached into the front of his car and fiddled with something, then knelt beside his front wheel. "Why not just drive it over there?" Exasperation sounded in her voice, as she didn't want anyone to happen by and see them. Even knowing no other traffic traveled there, she still thought about what that guy Murphy, whoever he was, said so long ago; If anything can go wrong, it will.

Mike looked at her like he wanted to throw something at her. Heaving a sigh, he said, "There are certain things one must do to get these things to go into the all-wheel-drive mode. You know, so it doesn't get stuck?" She detected a bit of sarcasm in his tone. "Just wait there and I'll be right back."

He slid into the car and drove off the road, slowly negotiating the hilly terrain to get it out of sight. She heard the engine stop, and a moment later he returned with a small carry bag, she guessed with his change of clothes.

She opened the trunk for him. He told her to drive slowly around the curves so she didn't toss him around. Getting back into her car, she muttered under her breath, "Yeah, I'll toss you around, asshole." She drove the rest of the way to her front gate and called for Manny to open it so she could go to the house.

"Everything alright, Wriley?"

"Just fine, Manny." She forced a bit of a smile. Her nerves almost betrayed her, but he let her in. She kept glancing into her mirror to make sure Manny didn't look at her as she drove up the driveway.

When she got to her garage, she pressed the button on the control and the door opened. She went in, closed the rolling door, then got out and popped the trunk open.

Getting out, Mike said, "Are there any cameras I need to worry about?"

"Not in here. I had the security people take them out after," her voice hitched a little, "after I got over my parents' death." Tears threatened to flow from her eyes, but she straightened her back and turned to march to the door. "I also had them disable all the ones in my personal halls and rooms. I think those perverts were watching me when they didn't need to."

She thought she heard Mike chuckle. When she looked, he still had the same serious look he usually had, so she led on. He followed her through the hallway and up some stairs, ending at a landing in front of a set of double doors painted mauve. She opened both and walked into a large room. The walls were painted a bright pink, the carpeting and bedding in darker shades, and there were stuffed animals everywhere. The whole room looked like it housed an eight-year-old girl, not a thirty-something.

She motioned him toward a side door. "There's a room in there you can sleep in." Her look suggested she wouldn't deny him if he'd rather stay with her. When he moved toward it, she said, "There's also a separate bathroom," sounding a bit hurt that he didn't give in.

He closed the door, so she began getting her things together to take a shower and get ready for bed. The phone on her nightstand rang, and she heard the chef on the other end when she picked it up. After assuring him she had already eaten dinner, she hung up and turned to find Mike at the end of her bed.

"Everything okay?"

She hadn't even heard him open the door. "Yeah, just the cook wanting to know if I wanted some dinner."

"I wonder how he knew you were home?" He looked around the room, then along the corners of the ceiling. "Are you sure about those cameras?"

"Yup." She would not be second-guessed by someone who had never been there before. "Manny probably told everyone still here that I'm home. As many times as I've done stuff I shouldn't," she walked by him toward her bathroom, holding her nighties in her hand, "I would have been reprimanded long before now if they had seen." With that, she slammed the door.

After her shower, she went back to her room, hoping

he had changed his mind about staying with her for the night. Her shoulders slumped when she didn't see him, and she pouted as she went and got into bed. She sat up and with a flourish, clapped twice to turn out the lights. She just loved that little convenience.

She had a bit of trouble getting to sleep, excited that she would have her cash the next day. That and the possibility they would get caught had her heart racing.

In her mind, she went over all the things she might have to say if things went wrong. She tried out one excuse, then changed it, rewording to get it right and abolish her of any blame. Talking her way out of jams seemed to be the one thing she could still do relatively well.

She drifted off to sleep. Her dreams centered on her standing atop a pile of money, a mountain of large bills that kept multiplying and falling from the sky. She had a laptop floating in front of her where she made purchase after purchase, but the pile kept building instead of diminishing. She ordered purses, shoes, clothes, pizzas. Anything she wanted would appear at the click of her finger on the pad.

She noticed some of the bills had a red stain on them. It didn't merit her attention, as she kept finding more stuff to order. The stains began spreading, the bills looking wetter with the red stains and she started trying to find where it came from. She couldn't see anything around the bottom of the pile, but the red kept getting on more of the cash.

When she saw a couple of drops fall right next to her, she noticed some on her shoe. She bent to wipe it off and saw it ran down her leg and followed the rivulet up. Then she felt a trickle on her neck. When she touched, it hurt a little, so she took her compact out and opened the mirror. Her throat had a wide gash, her own blood gushing out and running down to soak all her money.

How could she spend it if blood got all over it? She angled the mirror up and saw cuts all over her face.

She sat up in bed, frantically touching and wiping her face and neck. She looked at her hands, but they were dry. Tossing the sheets aside, expecting her bed to be covered in blood, she found a tangled mass of cloth from tossing and turning in the throes of her nightmare.

Swinging her feet off the side, she sat on the edge of her bed and ran her fingers through her wet hair. She stood and walked into the bathroom to splash some water on her face. When she looked in the mirror, she saw it covered in cuts again and recoiled in horror, wiping her hands across her cheeks and forehead, but the cuts were gone. No blood on her hands, nor on her nightie or the sink. She leaned on the edge of the lavatory, hanging her head and breathing hard. She couldn't remember ever having such a terrible nightmare before.

After drying herself and changing into a dry nightgown, she went to the door leading to the room she told Mike to stay in. Though mainly dark, she could see the fold-out couch bed had not been used. Maybe he had gone to find the best route to get to the safe in the basement.

She walked back to bed, doubting she would slumber anymore, but she fell asleep by the time her head hit the pillow.

She woke again with Mike shaking her shoulder. The sun had come up, making her room almost too bright. He pulled her to a sitting position.

"Wriley, come on. Wake up."

"What?" She still felt groggy. "What time is it?"

"Almost 8. Come on, I have something to show you." He stood and walked toward the door.

"Can I at least get dressed?" She noticed she had on a nightgown, but thought she had put on her sexy nightie last night, hoping to lure him into bed with her. Then she remembered the nightmare. "You wouldn't believe the dream I had."

"Tell me about it later. Come on."

"I need to put some clothes on."

"Time for that later, too. Come. On."

He sounded insistent, so she tossed on her flimsy robe and followed. He led her to a painting and stopped. "You've never seen as much mess," she started. He reached up and tugged on the frame and it swung on hidden hinges. "What? I never knew it did that."

"Yeah, I found it last night. Come on." He sounded a bit excited.

He stepped through and grabbed a rechargeable flashlight from its perch on the wall inside as she followed. He pulled the painting shut and led her down the dusty steps. They looked as if they hadn't been used in years, showing two sets of prints, one leading up and the other one down. When he spoke, his deep voice made a dull echo.

"I went looking around last night to find the best way to the cellar. Every time I tried to go down to the first level, I heard voices." So, she had figured right; he had gone looking for the safe. "Then, I found this passage. There are others, too."

She wondered how she had not thought to look for any. She had lived there her whole life and never knew there were ways to sneak around without being noticed.

They came to a landing and he stopped. "The next shift of guards will be in around 10. We don't have much time."

"The next shift? What happened to the night shift guys?" She knew there were three shifts. Normally three or four guards wandered the halls at intervals all night and day.

"I took care of them." She cocked her head. "You

could say I gave them the rest of the night off." He smiled, but it held no humor.

He pushed on the wall and it swung away from them, leading into her father's old study. When he ushered her through, it closed to reveal the bookcase where Daddy kept his business ledgers. That's why she would never find it from inside the room. She would not have bothered with any of those books.

She went over to the fireplace and looked up at her father's portrait. "How many more secrets did you have, Daddy?" She spoke softly, but Mike heard.

"More than you want to know," he told her and pointed to a pile of pictures on the desk.

She went over and saw the ones on top. There were photos of her, in her room with her hand wrapped around the pecker of her favorite "Uncle," one of her dad's friends who she had always been able to convince to buy her stuff. Starting on her 18th birthday, he began asking her to do "special" favors to make up for giving her what she wanted. She agreed but told him she just wanted the money, and she would buy her own stuff with it.

They had taken pictures of her doing so.

He knew the pictures were being taken, too. Several of the shots showed him looking toward the camera, making "Ooo" and "AH" faces, even pointing at her with one hand and giving a thumb up with the other as she concentrated on doing a "good job."

Those were not the only ones, either. Another "Uncle" had wanted her to "put it in her mouth," which she did so she could get money for a pretty bracelet she saw in the jewelry store. She had several encounters of that kind, and she couldn't say she didn't want to do those things. It excited her to find out how easy it could be to get loads of money from them. At first, she didn't like the mess they made at the end because they always wanted to do it all over her, but she soon expected it to be a necessary evil.

There were photos of every encounter. Some of them looked like they had been handled more, the edges worn and bent, others looked like fingers had been rubbed across them, especially the ones she had gotten naked for. Though she had never let one of them have sex with her, she had let some rub their cocks between her big titties. They seemed to like that the best.

As she pushed them around, she saw there were also pictures of her with her girlfriends. They would have sleepovers and run around her room in their see-through nighties having pillow fights or sitting in a circle playing "Truth or Dare," which more often than not ended with various girls getting naked and exploring each other.

She had been set up, and by her own father, so he and his friends could have naughty pictures of her and her friends doing stuff. Shame flooded her cheeks and tears fell from her eyes.

Mike stood behind her. "Oh, if you like those, you'll love this." He tossed some more pictures in front of her, but these looked more recent. They weren't of her, either. She recognized Samuel, one of the night guards. His face battered, his head no longer attached to his body. She recoiled and bumped into the man behind her.

She tried to turn, and his fist connected with her jaw. Her body flung forward, bending her over the desk as the side of her head banged on the unforgiving wood. Stars danced in front of her eyes and she saw his shadow walk around to the other side.

He grabbed her by the hair and pulled her over the top, most of the pictures sliding off and landing on the floor under her. He dragged her toward the hearth and pulled out the little dust shovel.

"You've been a very naughty girl for a long time, haven't you?"

He let go of her hair and she dropped, belly down and still a bit dazed. He pressed his foot to the middle of her back as he raised the shovel and brought it down on her ass.

"Does naughty little Wriley need a spanking?" He laughed without humor, raining punishment on her chubby ass for her past wrongs. While trying to get out from under his hold, she kicked and screamed "No!"

"No," he said as he tossed it aside. He rolled her over with his foot and grabbed her up by the front of her night clothes, throwing her against the bricks as he hoisted the poker. "I think you probably enjoyed getting poked when you were nineteen, didn't you?" He swung it hard and connected with the side of her knee.

She finally caught her breath enough to scream in pain. She swore she saw him bend his head back as a shiver shook him. He enjoyed hurting her, and hearing her scream more so.

When she started calling for help, he hit her again, the curved point sinking into her thigh. He pulled hard to tear a chunk of her skin open. She fell back to the floor with another yell for help mingled with sobs.

He dropped the implement and snatched her up again, pushing her onto the recliner. She remembered many times sitting on Daddy's lap while he held her, even after she had started doing things he had photographed. She had an errant thought of whether he had some illegal thoughts about her because of her indiscretions.

She looked at her attacker, holding her injuries as they bled through her fingers. "Why?"

Mike pulled out a thick document case from beside the chair and opened it toward her. Neatly stacked bills filled it. She couldn't estimate how much it held, but she suddenly knew she would not touch it. "You got me what I wanted," he closed the case and set it aside, "now I'll get what I need."

He walked to the wall and pulled a short sword from a display mounted next to the fireplace. She had always thought the weapons were fakes. She tried backing up the chair as he swung down and sliced off the fingers of her left hand. Her wails filled the room and she sank back down into the cushion, cradling her damaged hand.

Mike swung again, slicing into her upper arm, then again on her other side, her pleas for him to stop were drowned out by her cries of pain. He dropped the sword and leaned over her. His black eyes developed a fiery red center where his pupil should be.

"Poor, little Wriley. So concerned with getting more money that she didn't even care who helped her." He stood and walked to the desk, pulling the ten-inch long letter opener shaped like a little sword.

"Your dirty Daddy sure liked swords, didn't he?" He turned back to her, but she had used his temporary lapse to slide off the recliner and back toward the door, leaving a trail of blood.

He crossed the gap before she could get it open and flung her back to the center of the large room. She stumbled from her injured thigh and twisted her ankle, letting out another cry but not falling. She limped back until she bumped the bricks of the fireplace. He kept walking toward her, head lowered, glowering at her as he approached.

"You really are rich, Wriley," he told her. "Well, were, anyway." He raised the letter opener and swung it at her face, cutting her jaw and cheek. She put her uninjured hand up and he slit her palm open, then swung backhanded and cut her left eyebrow when she moved her hand away. He continued swinging, each time causing another wound.

He stopped after a dozen incisions littered her visage. She slumped to her knees on the floor, whimpering weakly, more tears flowing free from her eyes and stinging the cuts. She looked at him, hoping he had finished his assault, but he pushed her with his foot and she landed hard on her back.

He knelt and grabbed her left breast in his fist, then used a sawing motion to slice it off. Her right tit, he didn't even hold, just put the blade under the heavy bosom and pulled upwards. She didn't have enough energy left to scream.

He stood over her, barely breathing hard and splattered with her blood. "Now, how sexy do you feel?"

He removed another sword from the wall. A full-length broadsword with edges glinting as he half tossed it while spinning the hilt in his grasp. He looked back at her and lowered his head, his brow shadowing his black eyes. Using a two-handed grip, he swiped it along her neck laying open her throat. He took a step toward her, reversed the swing, and took her head from her shoulders.

The Chase

With Wriley dead and her millions in my possession, I had to get out of there with as much haste as I could. It wouldn't take long for the security forces scheduled to arrive soon to find what happened.

Throughout the night, I had searched the entire house, looking for ways to get around so I would not be noticed. I found the first hidden passage by accident.

On leaving Wriley's room after she fell asleep, I trailed my hand along the frame of a huge painting and felt a slight breeze. Closer inspection revealed a thin gap that should not have been there, so I started pulling the sides. It popped open revealing a dusty staircase leading down. A rechargeable flashlight hung on the wall, thick dust on it. I took it and closed the painting, then descended the stairway.

Each landing led to a different room. One let out in a large office, bookshelves lining the exit wall, a big fireplace on the side across from the regular door. There were collections of medieval weapons mounted neatly all around the walls. I left the section of the case I came through open so I didn't have to search for the hidden latch to reopen it and began browsing.

When I touched the displayed hangings, one of the short swords, showcased with another in a cross pattern behind a shield, came loose and almost fell to the floor before I caught it. I turned it in my hand, expecting it to be a non-lethal replica. The weight and balance were too accurate to be anything but a usable weapon. Placing it back in its holder, I continued my inspection.

I looked around the rest of the room as I continued toward the desk. I hoped to find the secret of the safe Wriley had mentioned so I could open it when the time came. I walked by some file cabinets and opened the drawers, glancing at the titles of the folders therein, looking in and seeing information useless to me.

When I got to the desk, I sat in the big leather chair and tried the drawers. All locked, so I looked through the items on top for the keys. In a decorative box, I found a stack of cigars. I had no interest in them but pulled one out. It crumbled with age. Upon closer inspection of the case, I noticed the lower portion looked like it would open. I closed the top and tried, with no result. Picking it up and turning it over, I noticed a small button. I set it back down and pushed it, rewarded with a click as the gap widened. When I opened it, there lay a ring of keys.

I began looking through the desk. Mostly what one would expect to find, assorted paperwork and receipts. One side contained miscellaneous files, an address book, and various office supplies. In the other row of drawers, I found quite the surprise.

The bottom one held a plethora of photographs, as well as the instant camera used to take them. I recognized Wriley right away. They were all of a pornographic nature, with her doing things with older men. It looked as if she had no idea the pictures were being taken, but the men involved did. Even in her late teens, she had been over-endowed and some of the men had taken the liberty of ejaculating on her as she pressed her big tits together.

There were also images of groups of scantily dressed girls, some involved in an innocent game of pillow fighting, others a bit more racy. Her father and his friends had a real perversion going on and the girl had no idea. There must have been another passage that led beside her room for her to not have known they were being recorded. I wondered if they had taken videos, too, but I didn't look for any.

I left a bunch of the pictures on top of the desk for use later. They would make a good distraction for when I brought her here.

In the next drawer up, I found the information I needed to open the safe. A small case, about the size of a business card. Etched inside, the word "Safe" followed by a series of numbers, and "Passage" with a four-digit code. Pocketing that, I looked inside the final drawer. Nothing in there concerned me, either, so I went back to the passage and continued down.

At the lowest landing, I found a metal door with a lighted keypad beside it. I blew on it to remove the layer of grime and took out the little case with the security codes. When I entered the numbers, the portal made a slight hiss as it released. I stepped through and found myself in the safe instead of facing it. The old man had his own entrance so he wouldn't be observed going to it by conventional means.

I went back up to the office to find a satchel. In the bottom bin of the file cabinet, I found a carry case designed for paperwork. I dumped the contents into the drawer and took it back to the safe. I didn't bother with anything but the larger bills, leaving stocks, bonds and the stacks of tens and twenties. I still filled it to the top, estimating at least a couple of million dollars in total.

When finished, I went back up and began tracking the guards. Morning would come soon, and I needed to be done and gone before the next shift of security arrived. I took one of the daggers mounted on the wall and went hunting.

I first went looking for the control room. There had to be one if there were cameras. I happened on the first man, who fumbled for his sidearm in his surprise just long enough for me to run at him and plunge the knife into his neck. As I continued sawing through the meat and tendons, his blood sprayed and sloshed, painting the wall, tabletop and the front of my shirt. I dragged him into the nearest doorway and found the monitors I had been looking for.

After disabling all the recording devices, as well as destroying the disks being recorded on, I went in search of the other three. One, I found sneaking a nap in the master bedroom, the king-sized bed soaked up all the life that drained out of him. The other two stood outside the glass doors of the balcony. I didn't know if they were watching for intruders or just stepped out for a smoke.

I opened the door with slow movements and caught the definitive scent of pot smoke. I grabbed both by the sides of their heads and smashed them together, sounding like two bowling balls colliding. They sunk as one to the floor, and I dragged them in and to separate rooms before driving the blade through their hearts.

When finished, I took them all down and into the safe, then went back to the office and got the same camera Wriley's dad used for his perversion and took some pictures to record mine.

Satisfied with my work for the moment, I went back up to Wriley's side room to clean up, wake the girl and finish so I could leave. I went in to shower and put on clean clothes, then packed all my belongings back in my small bag, looking around to make sure I hadn't forgotten anything.

As I entered her room, I heard her mumbling in her sleep, her covers looked like she had been tossing and turning all night. I shook her awake, but she acted very groggy.

"Wriley, wake up," I told her.

"What time is it?" She looked around as if trying to remember where things were. I noticed she didn't have the same night clothes on as when she went to bed but didn't concern myself with that.

"Almost eight. Come on, I have something to show you." I wanted her to know her father's perversion before she died. I didn't have a real reason, but it would entertain me.

She tried to insist on getting dressed, but I made her believe what I wanted to show her would be more important. She pulled on a light housecoat and followed.

I led her to the painting. When I pulled it open, she commented she knew nothing about it. I took her in and led her down to the study, telling her how I had found it and hinting my suspicion of other corridors.

When she asked about the guards, I omitted the particulars, telling her I "gave them the rest of the night off."

We went into the office and she stood in front of her father's picture over the fireplace. I heard her mumble, "How many more secrets did you have, Daddy?"

I walked up behind her and whispered, "More than you want to know," and pointed her to the photos I had left on top of the desk. She walked over and began moving them around. As she looked at them, she flushed with her shame. She obviously thought the acts were secret, even the ones of her with her friends.

"Oh," I told her, "if you like those, you'll love these." I dropped the pictures I took of the dead guards in front of her. She started to slowly turn to face me, but I hit her on the side of her face. She went down fast, and her head bounced on the top of the desk as I walked around it. I grabbed her by her blond curls and dragged her across the pile of photos, tumbling a lot of them to the floor.

I dropped her face-down in front of the fireplace and took up the small shovel meant to scoop the ashes, and brought it down on her big ass. "You've been a very naughty girl for a long time, haven't you?" I taunted her and laughed as I beat her, "Does little Wriley need a good spanking?"

I had another idea. Dropping the shovel, I hoisted her up and pushed her back against the bricks, then grabbed the poker. "I think you probably enjoyed getting poked when you were 19, didn't you?"

Stepping back, I reared and hit the side of her knee and she finally recovered enough of her senses to scream, her voice a lower pitch than Sharon's shrill screech. The sound reverberated through me, pleasure coursing through my body and causing a shiver to run down my spine. She started to call out, so I swung it at her upper leg and the side prong pierced her flesh. I pulled a chunk loose as blood flowed down her leg. She fell, sobbing and begging for help.

I let the poker drop to the floor and pulled her back up, then tossed her onto the leather recliner.

Through her tears and slobber, she asked, "Why?"

I guessed I would play along. I pulled out the briefcase I had placed next to the chair she sat on. "You got me what I wanted, now I'll get what I need," I said, showing her the contents.

I went to the display that held two short swords behind a shield and pulled one out. She began climbing the back of the chair, so I swung it down and relieved her left hand of the fingers. She howled again as she sank back into the seat. I sliced her twice more, cutting into the flesh of her upper arms, then dropped the sword and leaned over her, letting her see the fire in my eyes.

"Poor, little Wriley," I said. "So concerned with the money she didn't even care who helped her."

I went to get the large letter opener off the desk, also in the form of a sword.

"Your dirty Daddy sure liked swords, didn't he?" When I faced her again, she had limped toward the door. I got to her before she made it and threw her back to the center of the room, causing her to twist the ankle of her uninjured leg, but she didn't fall. She staggered back until she made it to the wall.

"You really are rich, Wriley," I told her. "Well, were, anyway."

I slashed her face a couple of times before she could raise her hand to block, then I cut deep into her palm. When she pulled her arm back, I swung over and over, giving her a dozen or so cuts. She would no longer be considered cute. In fact, it would take considerable work to give her an open casket burial.

She dropped to her knees and I used my foot to knock her onto her back. Grabbing hold of her huge left tit, I sawed it off, then placed the blade under her right and pulled up hard to amputate it as well.

I leaned toward her and said, "Now, how sexy do you feel?"

Her tears had to be stinging all those fresh wounds, so I decided to relieve her of her pains.

I walked over to a broadsword hanging vertically and pulled it down, spinning it in my grasp to test its weight. Returning to her, I swung it and sliced her jugular, then stepped up and, without ceremony, chopped her head off. Her blood gushed out like a fountain, pulsing with her heart until it slowed and finally stopped.

Time to go. Looking around the room, I decided to

take something as a memento. I thought hard about the sword I used to end Wriley's existence, realizing it would be a bit unwieldy. I also rejected the idea of the little letter opener. Mounted on the wall, I noticed twin daggers; ten-inches long and both edges of each sharpened. I tossed them both in the case with the cash and began my escape.

As I made my way through the hallways toward the back exit, I passed a door thicker than others I had seen in the house. Made of what looked like thick oak slabs with braces in a 'z' pattern bolted to it, I figured there might be something of value in there and decided to investigate.

Rummaging in my pocket to get the keys I had lifted from the desk in the office where I left Wriley, I found one that looked like it matched the locking mechanism. I slid it into the hole and turned, rewarded by the click of the latch releasing.

I pushed it open, rewarded by the sight of a room full of a wide array of weapons. Handguns and rifles mounted neatly across the walls, each according to caliber from what I could tell. I placed my small bag and the briefcase that held the cash next to the entryway and looked over the selections.

I didn't want anything large like a rifle, which would slow me down, so glanced over the pistols for one I could manage the easiest. Several of the semiautomatics had extra clips in a clear drawer under them and the revolvers had empty speed loaders in their bins. Along the floor, a slim, three-foot-tall cabinet had been built. Formica tops and wooden drawers, with glass doors under them showing shelves containing boxes of ammunition in every caliber and style for the weapons above.

I concentrated on the pistols with matte black finishes, not wanting the reflectiveness of chrome. I didn't want a revolver either, as they needed reloading too often. Glancing through the many variants, I concentrated on the ones with larger capacity clips, while also considering how comfortable they would be to hold. I didn't know much about brands or how accurate different models would be, so had to concern myself with ergonomics.

The one that felt right turned out being a 9mm semi-automatic with molded grips. The curves fit well, and the balance made it like an extension of my hand. I began looking at the various holsters that matched. I tried a couple of belt styles and some designed for concealed carry in the back of the waistline. None of them impressed me, as most were designed for right-handed shooters and I felt more at ease using my left.

I opted for a shoulder holster. I found it easy to just turn it around to make it left hand friendly, and it sported a double clip carry case. After grabbing every clip in the bin, I pulled out six boxes of ammo and set all the equipment on top of the counter. I did grab two double clip belt-mount carriers, then loaded as many bullets as I could and secured them in their perspective holders. I then started looking around for some way to carry it all.

A locker had been mounted to the wall behind the door. When I opened it, I found a wide array of jackets and various bags and cases on the floor. I flipped through the coats, some long and others waist length. Trench coats and windbreakers along with some that looked more like blazers and dinner jackets. I chose a trench coat, black leather that fit well and extended down to mid-calf, then grabbed a small collapsible bag from the floor.

As I placed all the equipment for the pistol into the bag, I saw out of the corner of my eye a row of shotguns. Several had pistol-grip stocks and had been sawed off, which I took an interest in. One of those would be easy to use in close quarters and have more devastating effects than a handgun. I pulled down a 12-gauge pump model and found 6 boxes of shells in the cabinet underneath. After loading it, I tossed the rest in the bag with the other items.

When I got decked out, I put the case containing the money in with the supplies and made sure there were no guards roaming the halls yet. Next to the door leading to the garage, I saw a peg strip with several rings of keys. When I opened the door, there were quite a few vehicles parked in neat rows. I snagged several key rings and went out, closing the door, and began viewing the choices for a getaway vehicle.

A little green British sports car caught my eye. All three of my hosts remembered the manufacturer, but none of them had seen a model with a hard top and hatchback feature; the popular models of the time all had convertible tops. I matched the key engraving to the car and discarded the rest, then opened the hatch and tossed the bag in.

The little 4-cylinder engine revved up on the first try, and I drove to the sliding bay door. Although I tried to open it silently, the disused rollers squealed as they turned, so I only pushed it far enough for the car to fit through.

When I drove out, I saw two guards who had heard the noise of the door and came to investigate. I sped toward them with intent to run them down. One dove to the side out of harm's way while the other tried pulling his sidearm, fumbling it around in his haste. I smashed into his legs sending him tumbling over the hood and roof. The one who moved rolled into a crouch while pulling his pistol but completed the movement too late to get a shot off.

I rounded the curve of the driveway and took the first

turn. I had seen a bit of the layout of the property from the balcony when I dispatched the potheads earlier and had a basic idea of which way I should head. The dirt road I followed would take me to a tract of warehouses. There had to be at least one I could use to prepare for the coming pursuit.

The first buildings I passed didn't have bay doors, but the third one did, so I veered in. The skies had clouded over, thunder announcing the threat of rain.

Leaving the engine idling, I hopped out and ran to the rear hatch to get more clips. Gathering as many reloads as I could carry, I confirmed they were full and dropped them into the deep pockets of the coat. I double checked the pistol, flicked off the safety, pulled the slide and eased the hammer back down before returning it to the holster, then made sure the shotgun held as many cartridges as it could hold and stretched to the front of the car to put it on the passenger seat.

The roar of an engine approaching told me time had run out. I slammed the hatch closed, slipped back behind the steering wheel, and exited the building, burning rubber.

I pulled out right as a big, black four-door car came around the bend. No matter how many times I weaved in and out of the spaces between the metal warehouses, he stayed right behind me. Several times, I saw the passenger try to lean out the window with his weapon drawn, but I didn't give him the chance to fire as I spun my wheel to take another corner.

Finally, I sped toward a tricky junction, it looked like about a fifty-degree acute angle to the right, that I knew would be difficult for the bulky car behind me to manipulate.

I spun the wheel and hit the brakes to fishtail so I could maneuver it, but the guy following me could not navigate the same and slid off the roadway into a ditch.

The skies decided to open up and rain came down in sheets. No warning sprinkles, just a sudden downpour. I couldn't see the next building, let alone the next turnoff, so decided to park the little car and try to lose them in the nearest warehouse.

I heard tires skid to a stop outside as I started trying to make my way to the opposite side of the room, hoping there would be another door. When I found that I couldn't see well in the darkness, I closed my eyes and took several deep breaths, trying to goad my sight to adjust. When I opened them, I could make out a maze of portable walls in the gloom.

Dripping wet, I made my way as quietly as possible through the cubicles looking for another way out. The main door burst open behind me and I ducked low to continue. The men who followed me whispered directions to each other and I heard the distinct crackle of two-way radios. It sounded like three had followed me into the office.

When I got to the exit door, I listened to get an idea of where the men behind me were. They seemed to be checking each cubicle they passed in case I intended to ambush them, but I knew as soon as I opened the door, they would know my location. With no option, I twisted the knob and pulled it open just enough to squeeze through and eased it shut.

I had entered a storage area, long emptied out and dusty. A jumble of boards had been tossed haphazardly nearby, so I grabbed a 2X4 and wedged it under the knob to delay the others when they got to it, then made my way to the open doorway leading back outside.

The rain had not let up. I turned up the collar of my jacket and ran into the downpour, crossing the driveway as I heard the board give way in the room I just left. They must have seen my silhouette through the downpour as three shots rang out behind me and one yelled, "Hey! Stop, you!"

I turned right when I reached the corner of another building and saw a large bay door. The rain pummeled the ground as I fled into the shelter.

Rapid fire explosions came from the upper level of the huge, almost empty space, causing me to scramble for cover as the swish of air announced the bullets missed by fractions of an inch.

I dove behind the nearest barrier, a stack of disused pallets, as the metal wall behind me screamed in protest of the lead piercing it instead of the human they had been fired at.

Looking through the gaps in the wood, I tried to see where the shooter hid, stealing glances over and around the side to pinpoint the origin of the shots. I couldn't even tell how many men were up there, just that they were intent on giving me a lethal dose of that hot lead for my deeds.

The pallets I cowered behind splintered as the offending projectiles impacted almost quicker than the noise of them being fired rang out. With each shower of debris, I ducked my head into my chest, the stench of fear assailing my nostrils, the humidity of my rapid breathing causing more sweat to trickle down my body. I almost marveled at how closely it mirrored the excitement of the kill.

During a short lull in the attack, I popped over the top to fire my pistol. I emptied the clip in short order, spreading the shots toward the aerial walkway supporting lights that shone directly into my eyes. Ducking back down, I ejected the empty and slid it into the pocket of my coat, replacing it with a full one.

I glanced around to try to find somewhere to relocate. Steel I-beams set throughout held up the roof. Skylights were staggered strategically in the roof for maximum illumination, though the dimness resulting from thick clouds and constant rain had activated the bright mercury-vapor lights.

The interior had been vacant long enough for dust to have settled in a thick carpet on the concrete floor. A few stacks of broken pallets and piles of lumber had been left scattered about, including the one I used as a shield from the relentless attack.

The protection offered by the blockade diminished as the bullets impacted. I saw a stack of plywood I could move to, but I didn't think I could make the entire distance in one dash. However, the support beam between the two hiding places looked large enough to use as a half-way point.

I counted; ten shots before the distinctive sound of a magazine being ejected and replaced by a full one. The reload took only a couple of seconds, but I thought that might be just enough to move to a new location. I needed to try to make my way toward the huge, metal sliding door to my left leading back to the gloom outside.

I wasn't sure what to do if I made it that far, but making a play for it seemed better than just crouching there waiting for a stray round to find a weakened spot and penetrate me instead of the wood.

As soon as I heard the last shot, I bolted for the beam. I barely made it before my assailant reloaded and the shots rang out again. They followed my path with shattering concrete and the whine of ricochets, accompanied by puffs of the thick dust covering the floor.

The ping of the steel beam being hit almost deafened me. I counted again and threw half of my current clip of ammo toward the shooter above as I prepared my dash for the next barrier. I knew that as I moved closer to my adversary, or adversaries, their accuracy would improve.

As I neared the reload count, I took several deep breaths, then bolted for the stack of plywood and dove toward the refuge as the shooting resumed. I landed on my belly and slid about twelve inches, then scampered the final distance and balled up into a fetal position as the shots impacted all around me.

The disturbed dust caused me to cough. In the back of my mind, I wondered what possible poisons could be mixed with it; what if it led to cancer? I figured I would not be so lucky to live long enough to find out, and almost snickered at the renegade thought.

The firing of my attacker ceased, followed by the clacking of hard soled shoes on metal stairs. It sounded like he intended to make it to the same exit I wanted so he could cut me off.

I rose and fired three more times, rewarded by a cry of pain. I dashed for the doorway, my rubber-soled boots making less noise than my labored breath.

As I burst into the cold rain, the pursuing shots resumed. I could only see two vehicles before the thickening downpour hid them. One, another black 4-door sedan, the other my green compact sports car. I could only guess the other cars I heard had gone to cover the entrance in case I made a run for it.

I looked back to see the shooter behind me, his limping gait slowing him considerably. I heard his gun fire, the hiss of the near misses followed by the thump of them penetrating the metal wall of the building behind the cars.

The window in the rear door of the gas-guzzler exploded beside me and I heard the plunk of another round as it pierced the passenger front door. With a prayer to the get-away gods, I fired my last shot into the front tire as I passed and hoped my acquired car gave me no problems starting.

I plugged the empty weapon into my shoulder holster and thrust my hand deep into my pocket for the keys. Wrenching the door open, I dropped into the little car, then slammed the door shut and glanced into the rear view to see my pursuer getting closer. I jammed the key home and turned it while mashing the clutch pedal, bouncing the accelerator to bring the machine to life.

Gunning the engine, I released the handbrake and popped the clutch. The satisfying crunching of rubber on wet roadbed rewarded my efforts and I fought the fishtail as I sped off. My last sight in the mirror showed the man beside his disabled transport. He thrashed his arms and stomped the hard, wet ground, no doubt accompanied by a string of obscenities as he bent to clutch his wounded leg.

I kept watch for another building I could pull in to so I could reload, eyes constantly scanning all sides and the mirrors. I had to squint to see through the thick sheet of rain all around. It would take a while for the gunner to fix the flat and resume the chase in such a deluge. Unless he decided to drive on the flat tire.

The building on my right had its door open, so I pulled the little car in. The parking brake ratcheted as I pulled the lever and killed the engine. I hopped out and opened the rear hatch, thankful I grabbed a supply instead of just enough for one magazine. The new rounds slid easily into the clips, though I had to concentrate to keep my hands from shaking.

The grinding steel-on-concrete scream alerted me to the approaching assassin. I dropped the hatch closed and leaped back behind the wheel.

The little four-cylinder kicked over, but the carburetor choked and failed to complete its job. I grumbled curses to the confounded god of misfortune, Murphy, who made the law that "if something can go wrong, it will."

Two, three times I turned the key back and forth, trying repetition and encouragement in addition to adjusting the choke lever and the curses I muttered under my breath, hoping to convince it I really needed to leave. Now.

"Come on, come on. Catch, you piece of..."

Finally, it coughed to life, just as the big, black nose of the town car showed through the murky downpour.

I shoved the shift lever into first and popped the clutch again, acrid smoke issuing from the squealing tires as I wrenched the steering wheel around and dropped the emergency brake handle.

I made two complete 360-degree spins before the big car aimed right at me, and I bolted away using the pungent smoke screen as cover, then spun the little car back around and shot toward the open door. It would not be long before the other driver realized the ruse and corrected his trajectory.

As I left the cover of the building, I glanced back in time to see the other driver had turned his wheels too sharply and the metal rim caused him to fail in the maneuver. The murky rain quickly concealed the view, but the resounding metallic crunch gave unmistakable evidence the chase would be delayed yet again.

I used the advantage to seek out another place to hide and gather my thoughts, maybe set up an ambush of my own. I could only hope the black car would be out of commission, at least long enough for me to get somewhere safe; or safer, anyway.

I glanced in the mirror again to make sure the tail hadn't returned. My attention shot back to the view ahead as a steel barrier materialized. Instinct and reaction could not avoid the crunch nor the sudden stop. Had I taken time for the seat belt, my head might not have impacted with the windshield, nor my chest with the steering wheel. At least, not as hard.

Dizzy, I pulled the door release. Disorientation settled in a fog as I rolled out onto the wet asphalt. I had to shake my head as I rose to clear the dancing spots of light behind my vision.

The rain had slowed as suddenly as it had started. I looked at the mangled metal, steam rising from under the hood with an insistent hiss as if it were telling me to be quiet. I hung my head and sighed, I had liked that jaunty little British car.

"A classic, and now it's ruined." I had to chuckle at myself. Of all the thoughts to have while trying to evade people who wanted to kill you.

Still smiling, I grabbed the carry case from the hatch, thankful I had found one large enough to hold the money bag as well as the extra equipment, but not so large as to be unwieldy. I lifted it over my shoulder and looked around to see which way to go.

I turned and made my way over the guardrail. My feet tried to disobey, but I stumbled forward, determined to be the aggressor again. As I negotiated the rocky slope, my strength ebbed, and I felt the need to sag to the ground. I made it to a small shelf and leaned against the cliff.

I needed a moment to figure out my next move.

Bruce Bellhouse

Jason pulled up to the gate and spoke with the guard on duty. It took a couple of minutes, then he came back to Beth's vehicle, bending low enough to get his jacket pulled over his head as best he could to protect from the deluge.

Beth rolled her window down a little. "He said his shift couldn't contact the overnight people," Jason hollered over the storm. "An intruder sped out of the garage in one of Mr. Canton's collection of classic cars and ran one of the guys down. They're chasing him through the warehouses." He handed her a two-way radio the guard gave him to monitor the activity. "Vic called Bruce, the man in charge, and told him I'm herre with a guest, so they'll be looking for us. He knows me, so we should be okay."

He motioned her to follow and they drove through, bypassing the main driveway and heading down a muddy track. She could barely see his tail lights with the sheets of rain obscuring everything, but he kept his speed down. Through some turns, they finally started passing some metal buildings.

They heard the team calling to each other over the two-way; they had found the green car wrecked at a guardrail along the flood control gully. No sign of the driver, but they were searching. A different voice, deeper, more authoritative, directed them into one of the larger buildings nearby so they could get a sit-rep.

The two newcomers went in and saw a big black sedan mangled by one of the supports. One of the men sat on a nearby pile of plywood, his pants leg cut up the side and a bloody bandage on his thigh. Another man came up to talk with Jason.

"Mr. Makeland." They shook hands and he gave a rundown of what they knew, which didn't amount to much yet. "I sent four men into the house to search. They'll have to do a room-to-room check, the man who went to Wriley's bedroom found nothing. We haven't located the night guards yet, either."

Jason introduced Beth and told him, "We believe he might have gotten into the safe and then killed her. Call in for the CPA to open it up."

"They should be here at 10, as usual. I'll have Vic call to see if they can get here sooner."

Bruce got on the radio, "Vic, Bruce here."

"Vic here. Go ahead, Bruce."

"Call the CPA. Tell them there could be a problem, so we need them to hurry their arrival. Let me know their ETA."

"Copy, Bruce."

"Jones, come in."

"Jones here. Go, Bruce." He sounded out of breath.

"I am on the way to your location with two guests accompanying me. Do not fire at the intruder until we get there unless absolutely necessary. Copy?" He began leading his contingent into the lessening rain.

"Copy, Bruce. We're at Building 23, copy?"

"Copy, Jones. Bruce out."

They walked toward the location of the wreck. As the rain let up a bit more, visibility increased. Beth didn't find it hard to believe Mike, or 'the entity' if Mike no longer controlled his actions, had crashed into the railing when obscured by the torrential downpour. The lanes between the warehouses were not very wide and had some tricky turns.

The muddy road that led through the various sized metal buildings stuck to her tennies in layers and made her feet heavy. "Glad I wore appropriate shoes for this," she called up to Jason.

He looked back and down to her feet and noticed that her white athletic shoes would not survive, the mud would soon overtake the tops and leak in. He took out his radio and called one of the men in the house. "William, you copy?"

"William here," came the static-filled reply, "go."

"This is Jason Makeland. I'm with Bruce and have a female friend with me. We didn't anticipate the weather. She's about the same size as Betty Canton. Can you run an old pair of her clod-hoppers out to the crash?"

"Roger, Mr. Makeland, on the way. Out."

Jason said something to Bruce and the two steered Beth into the next building. Not long after, a burly man came jogging in carrying a plastic bag. He handed it to Beth as his eyes scanned her small frame. He didn't even try to hide the lust in his gaze.

Bruce noticed how she began shifting herself away from William, her arms crossing over her small breasts and head bent low, and looked at him.

Stepping between them, nose-to-nose with his subordinate, he said through his teeth, "Stow that shit right now, Bill, or you'll find yourself in the unemployment lines trying for a dishwashing job."

William dropped his gaze and apologized. Beth took

the bag and sat to change. She tossed the soiled shoes into the same bag and thrust them into William's gut. "Dispose of these, would you, Billy Boy?"

She could see the anger enter his eyes. He didn't much like that name. Bruce gave him a non-verbal challenge, and he looked back down and mumbled, "Yes, Ma'am," as he took it and left. She heard various snickers from several of the others.

Bruce asked her, "All set?" She nodded, and they went to where the little green car had ended its run. The rain had lightened to a sprinkle and they could see down the rocky slope to where it dropped off.

"This place used to be a real flood zone," Bruce explained to Beth. "Mr. Canton had to have a lot of work done to make this control ditch, bringing in a whole lot of fill to build up this plateau and get it with just enough runoff slant so it didn't take the dirt with it. An engineering marvel, actually, and all his design."

Beth developed a bit of respect for the late Mr. Canton. "So how far down does this go?"

"About 250 yards straight down, but there's a shelf right past where it drops off that my men think this guy has made use of." He called on the radio for an update from those who had tailed the intruder to that point.

The report came in that they had lined the ridge at twenty-foot intervals, but had seen no movement.

"Bruce, William here," came over the speaker.

"Bruce here, go."

"We've just found Miss Canton. It's a real mess."

Jason hung his head. Bruce placed a hand on his shoulder to console him and responded, "Roger, William. Any sign of the night shift?"

"Negative, Bruce. CPA is due in ten more minutes to open the safe. Will report the findings. Over."

"Roger, William. Bruce out."

The rain had stopped. Steam began rising from the

rocks as the sun peaked out through the diminishing clouds.

Beth mused that the weather seemed rather fickle, and Jason, sadness tinting his voice, responded, "Yeah, you get used to it." Beth went to him and wrapped her arms around one of his.

"We kind of figured it this way, didn't we?"

He looked at her and straightened a bit. "Yeah." Regaining a little composure, he suggested that Bruce have one of his men to go down to the drop-off and try to get a fix on Mike.

Shots rang out to their right. Bruce ordered his men to stay there in case the intruder doubled back, as he, Beth, and Jason took off at a jog toward the activity.

They found two guards standing, weapons trained toward a cul-de-sac. "Report!"

"We had George go down to look, as ordered," an older guard said, "When he looked over the edge, the guy grabbed him and threw him off, then took a shot at us. Kevin shot back before I could stop him."

Beth asked to try to talk to Mike, and Bruce agreed.

"Mike? Can you hear me?" She hoped he would still answer to his name.

"Well," came the drawn-out response. "Beth Simpson. What the hell are you doing here?"

"Mike, I want to help."

Laughter reverberated the rocky hill. "Help? How do you figure on doing that? You gonna get them to let me go?"

A sudden shot rang out from below and Kevin toppled, a bloody hole in his temple. Everyone around dropped to hide behind the railing, Bruce grabbing Beth's shoulders and pulling her down as he shielded her with his body.

"Damn it, if you don't get him to surrender, we're going to have to take him out."

"Mike, please, stop!" Fear laced her plea. "They're going to kill you."

No answer came from below. Bruce called for his men to gather, then began giving orders in hand signals and his men moved in separate directions. He intended to block off the ledge on both sides preparing to take the man by force of numbers.

He told Beth and Jason to stay put. Jason started to object, and Bruce said, "My men have trained together. They can move as a team, but not if there is an unpredictable agent involved, let alone two." He looked at them both to let them know he had nothing against them. "You two stay here. As soon as we get him under control, you can come down. Understand?"

They nodded. As much as Beth wanted to be with them, to try to keep Mike from doing any more damage, she knew Bruce had a point.

Two men went off to the right, and two others backtracked to the wrecked car to inform the men already there what the boss had planned.

They would descend and follow the ledge toward the target. Bruce gave them enough time to reach their designated places, then took his three over the railing. They stopped just above sight of the walkway. When the men from the sides made their move, jumping out and calling for the killer to "Freeze" and "Don't move," Bruce and his men popped up to cover them.

The intruder had gone. Bruce pulled out his handheld, "William, Bruce here."

"William, go," came the reply.

"He somehow gave us the slip. Could be headed either to the house or the front gate. Tell your guys to keep a sharp eye out."

"Roger, Bruce. We'll keep watch."

Bruce looked at Beth, as she had caught up with them on the ledge. "Do not kill him," Bruce said into his handheld. "Wound him if you must, but do not kill. Understand, William?" The last of his statement carried a definitive order.

"Roger, Bruce. William out."

The leader then called the man at the gate, though he knew Vic would have heard the entire chase. "Vic, Bruce." Silence. That could only mean one thing. He called for William to go check on him.

"Bruce, William here."

"Bruce here, go."

"Vic's down," his voice quavered, but Beth couldn't decide if from sadness or anger, or both. "The son-of-a-bitch put a chunk of glass through his eye."

Both visitors turned their heads, but they did not show much surprise. "Gahdammit!" Bruce took a couple of deep breaths before answering, "Roger, William." As an after-thought, he asked, "Any sign of his car?"

A moment of silence, then, "Negative, Bruce. His car is missing."

"Roger, William." He had to get on this guy's trail before it went cold. Beth claimed that if he got away, more women would die. "All guards, load up and meet me at the gate. We have to find this guy. Bruce out."

He had already begun leading the group toward the guardhouse. When they all got there, Bruce took his forces aside to discuss events found in the house. Jason stayed with Beth, though she knew what they had found, the condition of the corpse.

The people from the accounting office arrived and were sent directly to the safe. Bruce gave instructions for them to contact him as soon as they discovered whether there was anything missing or not.

The reinforcements showed up in six black sedans and they finalized the plans. They figured the killer went back toward the casino, so that would be their destination.

Bruce told them, "He took Vic's radio, so he'll be monitoring us. We only broadcast what we don't mind him hearing. Understood?" The men agreed, and everyone took their assignments.

They loaded the vehicles with two guards in each, Jason and Beth taking the back seat of Bruce's lead car, in route to the gambling halls. He kept on the two-way, making sure the men left at the house knew what to do. They had to inform the police of the situation at the manor, but he decided not to let them know where the main force headed. Yet.

As they negotiated the twists and turns of the private drive, the announcement came over the radio of the findings in the safe. Half a dozen men lay dead on the floor. William informed them the killings must have been done elsewhere, for the small amount of blood in there. Security would have to move the bodies before the CPA people could get a tally on the cash, and that could not be done until the cops arrived.

They split up when they pulled into the lot to search for Vic's car. Bruce spotted it and called for the others to enter the building at different points and they coordinated so all of them would go in at the same time.

The other groups had gone into the main casino, while Bruce, William, Jason, and Beth went through the outer halls between the shops. They gave only cursory glances into the stores, knowing they would not find their guy, but hoping for some clue to where he had gone. When they met up with the others they all averred that they found nothing out of the ordinary.

A commotion from down one of the side corridors made several of them look. A black man came stumbling out, calling for help and in a tizzy. His eyes were wide, and he stood looking around calling for the police while he held up his hands.

Bruce initially dismissed him until he realized that

there was blood coating the man's palms. Casino Security had run over to him and Bruce moved in his direction as well. He identified himself and followed the three security men to the restroom, giving orders for the rest to wait and make sure no one else went in.

The Casino Security Police came out shortly after, faces ashen and disoriented. Beth understood why without being told. Mike had killed someone else.

They cordoned off the area by the time police and EMS arrived and Bruce shared as much information as he deemed necessary. The Law Enforcement Officers already knew of the situation at Canton Manor so some of the details he wanted to keep to himself had to be disclosed. Bruce omitted the fact that, since many of his own men were dead at the hands of this maniac, the situation had become more personal, though it remained a professional one as well.

Since the victim still had his company uniform on, it didn't take long to get a positive ID, even though his credentials had been taken.

A call to the tour bus lines revealed the vehicle stopped at a truck stop almost a hundred miles south of them. Bruce took his men and left, not waiting to explain the situation.

He sent one team back to the mansion to gather as much info as possible and told them to use cell phones only; no more radio usage. The remaining followed him as they took to the highway, going to the roadhouse.

Beth had a feeling more women would be dead by the time they caught up to Mike again. If they did. The bus he grabbed reportedly had over a dozen female passengers.

When they arrived at the travel center, the building had been emptied out and yellow warning tape had been stretched all around the entrances. Emergency vehicles sat with red, white, blue, and yellow flashing lights still on. People strained to see through and over the cops and paramedics, cell phones raised trying to get some gory footage.

Bruce made his way to the front to try to gain entrance, but they wouldn't let him through either. He found out which detective had authority and asked to speak to her.

"Detective Maron," he called out as she approached. The lady looked to be in her thirties, almost six feet tall and about 195 pounds. She had on a white button-down shirt and brown slacks, her black shoes looked like they had darker stains on the lower soles, obviously from investigating the room where the deceased lay.

Bruce talked with her about the recent situations and said he thought the same perpetrator might be responsible for her crime scene. She started to blow him off, but he called just low enough the crowd nearby couldn't hear, "Tell me, Detective, was her face sliced multiple times? Did the perp cut off her breasts?"

Maron stopped in her tracks. She turned and stormed back, grabbing the larger man by his collar. "Do you have something to do with this?" She seemed to be taking the brutality of the crime personally.

"No, Maron. We are looking for the same guy." He grabbed her hand and forced her to release him. "And it's not me."

She looked at him for a moment, then at those behind him, her gaze falling on Beth and staying there. "You," she said as she pointed at the young woman. "What's your part in this? It's obvious you're not one of them."

"Detective Maron," Bruce began, "we need to move this out of the public eye." He jerked a thumb over his shoulder, causing her to realize some of those wannabe reporters had trained their cells in their direction. She turned and motioned the group to follow, telling her people to secure the area and disperse the onlookers.

When they got inside, she began asking what they knew. Bruce offered what information he could, while Beth and Jason spoke in low tones to the side. "Did you actually see Miss Canton?"

"I didn't, no. William did." He brought William to the forefront to tell of what he found.

"That sounds like the same guy. William, follow me." She led him into the women's washroom while the others waited. They came back out and Maron verified to the others the similarities substantiated the probability the same person had been responsible.

She told them that security cameras outside showed thirteen other women had gotten back on the bus and they had continued moving south. She had put out a state-wide "All Points Bulletin" and a "Be on the Lookout For" on the vehicle but had gotten no hits as yet.

Detective Maron approached Jason. "So, what's your stake in this?"

"I met Beth when she showed up at the club where Wriley, the last victim, liked to go to. She had shown a picture to the bartender but didn't get much info, and I had seen the guy sitting with Wriley. Knowing Wriley had been trying to get her money, I figured this guy had agreed to help her, but I had a bad feeling about him."

He left out the parts about Allie and Joel. No one would understand that, and they would probably be dismissed as lunatics for suggesting some otherworldly entity had been at the heart of things. They hadn't even shared that with Bruce.

Maron asked various questions, trying to figure out what the perpetrator intended to do. She interrogated Beth as well. Something in her gut told her they weren't divulging all the information they knew.

"Why don't you people stick around? At least for the night, in case I need to speak with you again?"

"Fine," Bruce said. "Is there a motel nearby? We

need to get some rest, anyway."

The detective gave them directions to a seedy little dive not far away. The store had been evacuated, but since the group would need to get some food and drinks, she called the clerk back in to serve them.

They got what they needed and headed to the motel. Gathering in one of the rented rooms, they ate their makeshift dinner while discussing plans. Bruce decided they would check in with Maron first thing and get her to clear them to leave, reminding her that they could traverse county and even state lines if necessary, while her department would be bound by territorial lines and procedures. The red tape involved with her trying to chase and apprehend the suspect would give the guy time to get away, allowing him to kill again.

Everyone went to their assigned rooms after they finished. Though they didn't have clothes to change into, Beth suggested they at least shower. The smell of so much sweat almost made her gag. Bruce had been humored by her remark, but gave in and told the others to hang their shirts to let them air out after they cleaned up.

Detective Susan Maron

Susan Maron hated certain parts of her job.

She had been with the County Sheriff's Department for twenty years, most of which she had worked patrol as a deputy. Five years ago, the Sheriff reluctantly gave her the position when his senior detective retired. Maron had been the only one who showed the determination to advance, not to mention the ability to perform the job.

There were two other women in the ranks of deputies, but females rarely stayed around long enough to be advanced past patrol. Mainly because of the torment and sexual harassment the men put them through.

Susan, at 5'9" and 190 pounds, didn't get the usual propositions. She had never been considered attractive. She had wiry brown hair, not even shoulder-length and usually pulled back in a small ponytail and hidden under a cap. Her brown eyes had not tempted anyone to stare into them and her complexion left a lot to be desired.

She heard all the lesbian remarks and jokes, even put up with the accusations of being a dyke. She allowed them to think what they wanted, for she didn't have any reason to prove otherwise. No one in her department warranted her affections. She concentrated on doing her job, and she did it well.

The sexual harassment towards the other women ran thick. Most of the men on the force were no more than hicks and bullies who abused the authority, each on a power trip as they hid behind the badge. Few had the integrity to make thorough, impartial investigations.

Maron, however, didn't put up with their bullshit. She had been reprimanded a few times, but when such cases arose, the men involved always fucked up and flew off the handle, proving her in the right. She got a lot of flak from them, but they had figured out she was not the one they wanted to tangle with.

As not much happened in the sparsely-populated county, she still had to patrol the highway, handing out citations for moving violations and taking care of shoplifters at the travel center. At times, the truck stop gave her more business than the travelers did.

There were the occasional murders, though. Truckers who were hyped up on the current version of speed or meth, taken to extend the time they could be on the road, usually had short tempers. Fights were a regularity, either in the store or on the lot. Most went unreported.

She shared duties with one man, Detective Tom Harris. He, however, had a drinking problem and would usually just follow her lead, even though he had seniority. That gave him more time to sit in his car on the side of the road or at a rest stop hitting off the bottle of honey liquor he kept in his glove compartment.

The call came in just after lunchtime. She had left June's Diner moments before, the grilled chicken sandwich and fries she regularly feasted on sitting firmly in her stomach. Dispatch came on and told her there had been another incident at the truck stop. A woman had been murdered in the restroom.

When she got there, the condition of the body had taken her by surprise.

Susan had never seen a case involving mutilation. She expected to find some woman strangled, stabbed, or shot, as those were the preferred methods she had witnessed in the past. The lady who found the body, as well as the black man who tried to help when she came out screaming and crying and several of the responding deputies, had not reacted well to the scene, their vomit splattered in the trashcan or in the sink.

After being warned to prepare herself, she herded the others out so she could examine the evidence. The woman sat in the last of three stalls. Her feet, slack and pointing inward, were visible under the door. When Maron pushed it open, she fought to not unswallow her recent meal.

She turned her head, bringing her left hand up to press her finger under her nose. When she regained her composure, she looked back.

The victim had been dragged in and her blouse had been torn open, then her brazier cut in the middle. Her breasts had been sliced off and her neck had been cut. It looked as though the perp held her over the bowl when he sliced her throat, as not much blood hit the tiled floor other than what had flowed from her chest. Maron shifted the body to the side and found the detached breasts floating like two huge fleshy turds in the bloody water. Rigor mortis had set in making the body almost as stiff as a board, so she knew several hours had passed since her death.

Maron backed away until she bumped into the far wall. She turned to grasp the sink next to her, looking at her own reflection and glancing at the image of the body behind her. She then ran some water into her cupped palms and wet her face a couple of times, grabbed some paper towels to dry off, and went out to talk to any witnesses.

No one had seen anything until the unfortunate woman who made the discovery had gone in to relieve herself before getting back on the road. She came out screaming, and two of the truckers went in. One threw up in the sink, then the call to 9-1-1 had been placed.

"I was driving from mid-Arizona to my home in Western California after visiting with relatives for the weekend," she stated. "I stopped at the store to fill up and get some refreshments, and when I went into the restroom, there was a nasty smell. I couldn't breathe and thought maybe a wild animal had gotten in and died, it was that bad.

"When I got to the last stall, I saw the feet of that poor woman. I knocked and called, asking if she was okay, if she needed help, but didn't get an answer, so I pushed the door open. That's when I saw," she couldn't finish, as she broke into tears again.

The ambulance had arrived and Maron called them over to take care of her. One of the paramedics asked, "What about the victim?"

"Nothing we can do for her, and this lady needs attention," Maron told him.

Talking to the store clerks, she got no more valuable information, so asked to see the surveillance tapes. She hoped those would be more useful. That's when the entourage of big men, accompanied by a small, lithe young woman and a guy who looked well-to-do, came onto the scene with their tale.

Maron didn't know how to take their story. It seemed illogical for someone to just go around abducting women and cutting off their tits before killing them. There had to be more to the story; something the people weren't telling her.

The recordings showed four camera locations in a split screen. She went through the tapes and found the time frames she needed, starting with the victim entering the toilet and the huge man that followed her in. She then backed the recordings to see the start of their visit.

The small tour bus stopped at the front of the store, doors opening to let a string of women off. Maron counted 14, all looked to be the same body type as the dead woman in the bathroom.

The bus then drove around to the pumps and the driver, 6'3", maybe 200 pounds wearing a long beige trench coat and dark, wrap-around sunglasses, filled the tank and went into the store.

He walked around and gathered various items; a couple of small baseball bats, like the rig drivers used to check the pressure in their tires, several rolls duct tape, and a package of string or rope. He went to the register and paid in cash while he had a discussion with the cashier.

He took his purchase out then used a different entrance to go back inside the store. Maron had reached the spot she started the tapes from. The woman had gone into the bathroom and the big guy went in after. Five minutes later, the man came out and went back to climb into the tour bus.

He drove around to the main entrance just as the other passengers came out, and they filed in. The tour bus drove away, heading east. From that, she surmised they might be headed towards Las Vegas.

Detective Maron asked to speak with the cashier involved. Bobby, a twenty-year-old who lived not far from the store, had come on duty just before the incident. His eyes drooped with exhaustion, but he tried to recall the conversation. He remembered the guy not only because he had paid cash for a company vehicle, but the other items he purchased, too. They didn't seem like the kinds of supplies a small tour bus would need.

"The big man had said something about trouble with

the banks, so they gave him cash to pay for supplies. I thought it strange, but when you work at a place like this, you see a lot of strange stuff. I just blew it off, ya know? It's not really any of my business."

Maron felt like giving the kid an earful but realized he was right. Seeing the kinds of people who filtered through that place daily would get old after a while. So many stories they would end up sounding much like the next one. She told him, "Alright, go on home, but let me know if you think of anything else," as she handed him her card.

It had been a long day. Maron decided to go home herself and get some sleep. In the morning, she would get with the group she had sent to the motel and try to get some more information. The son of a bitch responsible for this had to be stopped, and she hoped he would put up a fight rather than giving up peacefully.

On the Run

A female voice called out, "Mike? Can you hear me?"

I knew who it belonged to. "Well, Beth Simpson. What the hell are you doing here?"

"Mike, I want to help."

I had to laugh. Maybe I could use her efforts as a smoke screen. "Help? How do you figure on doing that? You gonna get them to let me go?"

Looking through a gap in the rocky slope, I took aim at one of the men above and squeezed off a round. The bullet hit its mark, and the guard went down with a hole in his temple. The others dropped out of sight and I made a break back toward the spot I had descended.

I heard Beth calling again, but refused to answer and give them my location.

I kept following the ledge, looking for either a way down or back up. It wouldn't take long for them to organize a rush to where they thought I hid, then they would know I had slipped away. I needed to be gone before that happened.

I came across a pathway leading along the side of the man-made drainage slope. From the location, I figured it would take me close to the entrance gate. The guard there would probably have his car nearby. I could use that to flee the premises.

Keeping low, I maneuvered close to the shack, listening to the radio chatter coming through the open window. I glanced over the sill to see the guard looking at two monitors hoping to see some movement. I moved around to the opening and dashed in.

I hit him in the back of his skull with the butt of the pistol and he went down. His head shattered the glass in front of him. When he rolled to the side, he had a large sliver in his right eye, blood gushing down his face and neck.

I went through his pockets and got his keys out, wiping them as best I could to get his piss off them, then decided to take his radio to keep tabs on the progress. He drove a black coupe with dark tinted windows. I tossed my bag of supplies in and drove away.

By the broadcast, I knew they had made it to where they thought I'd be and figured out that I had left the area. They called to the men in the house to tell them to watch for me, then tried the one I had just killed.

"Vic, come in," came a deep voice. I pressed the accelerator a little harder, not wanting too much speed lest I slid off the road and make their job easier.

The voice tried twice more to raise the dead man, then called to one in the house to investigate, saying they were heading in that direction.

"Bruce, William here," came the next call.

"Bruce here, go."

"Vic's down. That son-of-a-bitch put a chunk of glass through his eye."

I could imagine Bruce saying *Damn it!* "Roger, William. Any sign of his car?"

"Negative, Bruce. His car is missing."

"Roger, William. All guards, load up and meet me at the gate. We gotta find this guy. Bruce out."

I had made it back to the main road and turned toward the casino. I needed to find a way out of town.

When I pulled into the lot, I saw a small tour bus. Several women milled about as the driver loaded up their cases and bags in the storage compartment. All the 'ladies' I saw were of the dimensions I considered needing alteration, and I knew my next move. Looking in the glove compartment, I found a pair of wrap-around shades with dark tint. Coupled with the long overcoat, I figured I'd fit right in.

I parked nearby and tailed the driver into the lobby. He walked into the restroom and I followed. As he stood at the urinal, I came up behind him and slammed his face into the wall. His blood splattered, and he went limp. The amount of excrement that flowed out made me think he'd chosen the wrong stall to use.

I dragged his fat ass into a stall and wrestled him onto the toilet. Opening his outer shirt, I tore a piece off his undershirt and wet it at the sink to clean the spot off the wall. That done, I took his credentials and keys, then walked out to the bus.

The passengers had loaded up and sat jabbering to each other as I boarded. "Ladies," I began. They quieted, looking at me then out the window for their driver. 14 characters for my next games.

One of them stood and asked, "Where's Chuck?" The driver's card listed him as Charles Ramber.

"Chuck got an emergency call and had to go." I gave my best smile to allay suspicion. "The company sent me to replace him and told me to let you all pick your next destination."

"That's highly unlikely," the same woman said. "Let me see your ID." This one would be trouble. As she approached me, I pulled down the dark shades and glared at her.

"That won't be necessary, will it?" I spoke soft but let the fire in my eyes flare. She backed off, not taking her fear-widened eyes off me, and resumed her seat.

"Can we really pick our destination?" Another one spoke up, sounding a bit inebriated despite the early hour.

"Absolutely. Anywhere you want to go, I'm authorized to take you."

Most of them spoke together, and the decision came out in a single, multi-voiced cheer, "Vegas!"

I smiled. "Las Vegas, it is, then. Drinks are in the fridge in back," I saw the compartment when I came on board, "and the Wi-Fi is on. Sit back and enjoy the ride!"

I sat down and started the engine. I still had the two-way and knew the forces were about halfway to the casino. I pulled out and headed east, with no intention of getting this load where they wanted to go.

Their incessant chattering covered the noises from the radio after I had lowered the volume, and I heard the group from the estate had reached the casino and found Vic's car. A search of the building had ensued, which would take hours unless someone else found Chuck for them. I turned the radio off and dropped it in my equipment bag.

I could not only see but also heard the trouble-maker talking to others as I looked in the mirror, trying to convince them something might be wrong, telling of what she saw when I lowered my shades. Most of the others just brushed her off, but a couple cast apprehensive glances my way.

We neared a truck stop, and I called out asking if any needed a potty break. Half of them either raised their hands or said "Yes," so I pulled in. I decided to fill the tank up and told them to meet me out front in an hour, giving them enough time to grab something to eat and me enough to get rid of the instigator.

After they filed out and into the store, I drove around to gas up, then went in to search for some items I needed. I got a couple of tire thumpers in the shape of small baseball bats, several rolls of duct tape, and a package containing 50 feet of clothesline.

The cashier gave me a strange look but rang it all up. I paid cash, which earned me another questioning look, so I said, "The company is having an issue with the bank. They gave me some paper money so I wouldn't have to use the card while they straightened things out." I gave the guy my best smile and he shrugged, thanking me for my business, then I took the items to the bus. It didn't seem like a busy time for gas, so left it there and went back inside.

I spied the instigator moving toward the bathroom and went up behind her. Clamping my hand over her mouth, I pushed her into the women's room and locked the door. She struggled, twisting and turning to escape my hold, but I tensed the arm I wrapped around her chest to make it hard for her to move and breathe. I had my left hand over her mouth and nose; I just had to wait for her to pass out so I could do my business with as little resistance as possible.

She went limp in my arms, so I dragged her into the back stall and plopped her down. Too bad I had to render her unconscious. I bet she would have had a marvelous scream, but I couldn't afford that much noise.

I ripped open her blouse. Taking out the dagger I had kept from Wriley's, I cut the middle of her bra to expose her over-sized melons. I had to make it quick so I wouldn't be gone too long, I didn't have time to remove her head, as I had for the others, so I just pulled her off and leaned her head over the throne to slice through as much of her neck as I could with one strong movement, letting her blood fill the toilet. Then, without ceremony, I sliced off one bosom, then the other and dropped them into the bowl. Afterward, I found it a chore to get her to sit properly but finally got her position right so she didn't slide off.

Before I could go back out, I needed to clean the blood off my hands and hide the stains on my clothing. After scrubbing, I exited the bathroom and went back to the bus. I drove back to the entrance to wait for the gaggle to return. They trickled back out, all gossiping between one another. I had counted how many got off, and when I had them all back, I closed the door and resumed the journey.

About half an hour later, I heard someone say, "Hey, where's Janice?"

"She decided she didn't want to go on," I hollered back. "I got her a ride with a trucker to the bus station so she could go home." Most of them seemed to accept that. What a gullible bunch. I needed to watch the ones she had infected with doubt, though.

I turned south on the interstate. The women didn't notice immediately, but when one did, the others chimed in.

"What's going on?"

"Vegas is the other way."

One got up and came to the front. "Where are you going? Are you stupid?"

I pulled over to the side of the highway and stood, towering over the new bold one. "Sit your fat ass down." I had a growl in my voice and she began cowering but didn't move away.

"I want off," she said softly.

"Fine." I turned as if to open the door, but swung around with a backhand and laid her out in the aisle. The rest went silent. "Anyone else want off?" Various whimpers and sobs answered me. I couldn't afford any more of them getting brave, so I pulled out the clubs. "I need you all to go to sleep now, while I find a place to play with you."

Most of them had gone wide-eyed. I began with the front seats and walked through, swinging the cudgels at every head to knock them senseless. I wielded the bats with ease, back-and-forth swings conking each either in the back of their skulls or on top, each one sounding like a line drive. The arms and hands thrown up for protection got the bones broken, and their noggins were knotted, anyway.

When I got to the rear seats, I heard a couple who had not gone unconscious with the first hit, so made my way back to them and rectified it. Several of the blows broke skin and soaked hairdos red, but it looked like they were all still breathing.

I sat back down and drove on, looking for a side road I could travel down to find a secluded spot to take care of my business.

Desert surrounded the interstate highway, and sparse traffic made my trip easier. I saw a dirt road to the right and slowed to turn on it. I couldn't see any fresh tracks, so figured it would be lightly traveled if at all.

I drove for ten miles before I saw another track to turn on. I couldn't see the highway anymore and the two buildings I had passed were nothing more than shells.

In the distance, I saw a large house. As I neared, I saw the roof looked about ready to cave in. The outer walls had slats missing, the windows were mostly broken, and the front door hung on one hinge. It did, however, look to have plenty of rooms. Maybe it had been a mansion at one point in time, set a fair distance away from the maddening crowd, as it were.

I parked next to it and made sure my guests were still out. I needed to investigate and make sure no one had been using it for a crash spot or a party house. I knew how "kids" were.

All the trash that littered the property were covered in thick layers of sand. The inside looked as run down as the outside did.

Satisfied with the seclusion, I began carrying the girls one by one into separate rooms. I took the tape and rope in and began tying them up, binding feet together and hands behind their backs and wrapping tape completely around their heads to cover their mouths. I cut a strip of cloth from their clothes to cover their eyes, then used more tape to secure it in place.

I didn't have the right kinds of tools to use, so needed to go get some. I also figured I needed to get rid of the bus and get something smaller. I knew most modern fleet vehicles would have some way they could be tracked. Besides, when I got back on the road, I would only need enough room for me.

After taking some precautions to make sure none of the bundles could wriggle free, I hopped back into the bus and went to find another truck stop. I knew someone would have found Janice by then and the authorities had been contacted. They might have surveillance footage of me and the bus, not to mention how many others I transported.

The men searching for me might make it to the first stop and be able to find out which direction I went. When they got to the second, I wanted them to find the bus, blood and all, but not be able to do more than guess what happened between stops and where I went from there. I doubted they would realize I hadn't killed the passengers yet, but instead doubled backed to finish them off. They would most likely believe I continued on in the same direction.

Coming to an old gas station, I pulled in and around back. I kept glancing at the top of the light poles and around the edges of the building to locate any cameras. As I hoped, the place predated video monitoring. I pulled around back and parked in the middle of some other buses, all decrepit and long abandoned.

Making my way to the front, I watched for a vehicle I could commandeer. The trick would be to find one that hadn't been left there for servicing and, at the same time, parked out of the line of sight from the inside. I didn't need to be observed.

I saw an older fellow, mid-sixties or so, finishing filling his long 80's-era sedan up, then pull away from the pumps, parking on the far side of the station before going inside. I figured he would be in there for a while, else he would have left it at the pump while he paid.

I went around the back of the building and picked up various implements that had been tossed aside or dropped so I could have some toys for my new friends. Some broken pry bars, bent saws, and a sledge with half a handle would be good enough to use.

When I got to the car, I tried the driver's door. He hadn't locked it. Why should he? Nothing probably ever happened around there. I tossed the tools and my carry-all into the right-side foot well and sat in the seat, then pulled down the visor to see if he'd put the keys there, but came up empty.

When I got back out, I noticed a flash under the seat. Reaching down, I pulled them out, he just dropped them beside his leg when he parked.

I started the vehicle and verified it had a full tank, then decided I should grab some items from the bus; drinks and snacks to keep up my strength. I drove behind the building and parked near enough to the soon to be abandoned transport to make a hasty getaway if needed. I still wanted to avoid being seen, so drove slowly out the far driveway.

When I got back to the mansion, I went room-to-room to check on my guests. Most had awakened and were squirming to get free. One had almost gotten her feet free of her bonds, so I decided to start with her. I had been walking softly so they wouldn't know I had returned and set down my bag. After taking off the trench coat, I pulled out the sledge.

She finally got her feet freed and rolled onto her side to work on her hands. Her thrashing legs bumped against me and she froze, not knowing what she hit. I squatted beside her and touched her shoulder. She recoiled, then began to try to scream. I pushed her back over and straddled her, sitting my 190-pound bulk on her flabby belly. I knew she wouldn't be able to breathe well with me on her like that.

Setting the hammer down, I withdrew one of the daggers and began cutting the tape covering her eyes so she could see. When I pulled it away, she winced from both the brightness of the late day sun and the removal of some of her eyebrows. I gave her a second to focus on me, tears beginning anew, then grabbed the hair on top of her head. I lifted and pulled the tape around, taking my time so she felt each blotch of hair that went with it. She started crying louder as it ripped more out, then her noggin thumped on the floor as I let go.

She wagged her head back and forth, her legs still thrashing as she tried to get out from under me. I leaned close and told her, "I'm going to take the tape and gag off now. I want all your friends to know I've returned and begun my games. They'll hear your screams, and when they stop, each one will wonder if she's next."

The woman still wouldn't be still enough for me to get the blade under the adhesive, so I sliced her cheek. She tried to call out, her sobs coming through her nose along with a lot of snot. I grabbed her chin and forced her to look at me.

"Next time, I might miss and slice your throat. Is that

what you want?" Her fear had her shaking her head "no," so I told her to be still.

When I got her gag off, she began with her pleas. Hers were like all the rest had been, "Why are you doing this?" "Please let me go!" and of course, the age-old, "I won't tell anybody." I treated them like rhetorical questions.

Since she had gotten her feet free first, I decided that would be the best place to start. Speaking loudly enough for all of them to hear, I declared, "Listen up! I have brought you all here for a little game. I want you all to know that no manner of pleading or bargaining will spare you my attentions, and might just make matters worse.

"I'm starting with," snapping my fingers and cocking my head to the side to let her know I hadn't gotten her name, I bent closer. "What's your name again?"

She seemed to think I would soften if I knew, like knowing about her would create sympathy, for she said, "Rose. My name's Rose Parton. I have," my laughter cut her off. She looked a bit confused that I would laugh.

"I beg your pardon," I began, and saw fear replace the hope as I raised the sledge with one hand, as I continued in a bit of song, "I never promised you a Rose Parton." I guffawed as I brought the steel down onto her left knee. Her scream vibrated the old wood and some dust filtered down from the beams.

Looking at the falling particles, I said, "That's quite a scream you have there, Rose Parton." I figure since I would be the last one she would hear use her name, I might as well use it as often as possible. "Have you considered trying out for a part in a horror movie?"

I laughed again at my own joke and swung the sledge down on her other leg, catching her shin and shattering both bones there. She passed out. "Oh, darn." I spoke loud for the others to hear again, "I'm going to have to find another participant since Rose Parton has gone to sleep for a little while."

I moved from room to room, stopping at the door to each and asking if the resident wanted to be next. "Aw, nobody wants to volunteer? Take the chance to give someone else time to try to get away?" Since no others had been able to get any of their limbs freed, I didn't feel too concerned about it, I just wanted them to keep some hope it might be possible.

I picked a room at random and took one of the rusty saw blades in with me. Kneeling with my knees on each side of her head, I used the tiny sword to cut her gag first. As I pulled it away, I covered her mouth with my hand and announced, once again for everyone to hear, "By the way, I'm not letting anyone go, so don't ask. I'm also not going to give a reason for doing this, so that doesn't need to be asked, either." Speaking to the one in front of me, I said, "Understand?" She nodded agreement.

I removed my hand and began taking her blindfold off, then pulled her head up and yanked both strips away. Her hair had stuck to the tape, too, as I knew all of them would, and she screamed in pain as it ripped out of her scalp. Her voice sounded even more pleasing than Rose's had, but didn't affect the surroundings.

Dread shone in her orbs as I stood and held up the rusty saw. I called out, "Since I only have a limited number of toys, some of you will have to accept one I've used on someone else. Don't think you're not special to me, though," and I looked at her directly, "you all are special." I knelt beside her and grabbed her right tit. Placing the serrated edge against the shirt covering her, I tensed my arm. "I just love to hear you..." and pulled the blade hard.

The fabric tore, the blood gushed; her shriek sent more pleasure down my spine. I finished sawing through her flesh and, though she had gone unconscious, followed through by doing the same on the other side. I almost lamented not being able to give each one the attention they deserved, but I couldn't spend too long despite the remote location.

I decided to remove her head without waiting for her to wake since she had pleased me right away. That way I could move on to the next. I still had eleven more of them untouched. The action with the dull saw took a little longer and made a whole lot more mess, both in the room and on me.

Rose had begun moaning so I returned to her. I might as well get the entire process done with each, so I didn't accidentally forget to go back to one. Better safe than sorry.

I still held the saw, glistening with blood and littered with bits of flesh. Rose fluttered her eyes open and they roved in her sockets as she came to. I knelt back down to her as I came into focus.

Before she had much time to react, I jammed my fingers into her mouth and grasped her lower jaw. Stabbing the tip of the saw into her mouth, the flesh of her cheeks stretched far back in an almost comical grimace before reaching their limits. I had to make exaggerated movements to cut through the loose skin, ripping instead of slicing to the back of her jaw until I hit the skull. She had wailed throughout the process.

I changed hands and placed the gore-laced serrations against her neck. Her eyes went wide as I pulled hard and severed her windpipe, then watched as her artery stretched each way as if avoiding the inevitable outcome. I put more strength into the next forward cut, and the not-so-sharp teeth finally penetrated. Dark red blood sprayed in a semicircular arc, pulsing with her rapid heartbeat and coating me even more.

When I tossed her dismembered noggin to the side, I

stood and wiped my hand down my face to fling the thick coating off. "Okay," I announced. "I'm going to take a break now. You gotta believe, this is a lot harder than it looks in the movies." I laughed again as I walked back downstairs and out to the car.

I grabbed the bottle of water I opened while driving and used it to partially clean the blood from my face. Looking at the state of my clothes, I shook my head. I only had one more clean change, so I'd have to get into the ones soiled from Wriley's house when these became unwearable.

I got one of the beers and chugged it, letting out a healthy belch when done. I decided to take some of the little bottles of booze to give the remaining girls something to help them rest, for it would be a long night for them. Taking another beer for me, I went back in.

I strolled down the hallway, looking in on them as I announced, "Ladies, the sun is about to set. I'm going to have to make quick work of two more of you before it gets too dark for me to see. Like I said, these games take a lot of work.

"The good news is, for those who get to wait until tomorrow, I have a special surprise to give you, to help you sleep." As I made my way up and down the corridor, I made deliberate thumps with my steps, so they would know when I walked past their room. "You won't know which are gone and which remain, but if I give you your present, you're good until sunrise."

I ceased making noise as I went into each room to decide whether to take or leave the occupant. When I finished viewing all of them, I decided which would make it, and which wouldn't.

Those who had already soiled themselves were more likely to make it until morning, as they were already in fear and would suffer more than the rest. Three of them had been able to keep their bladders and bowels under control, so I would give them the business.

I took up the little hatchet I found behind the garage and tested the weight. I went up to contestant number three and watched as she strained her ears to find out where I ended up. I wouldn't bother taking the tape off, as darkness deepened with each passing moment.

I hoisted the tool and slammed the jagged edge down on her neck. Another fountain rewarded my efforts, but I couldn't wait for it to stop, I had to move on. The next two brave ones had rooms next to each other, so I walked between them trying to decide. I didn't want to do the same to all of them, I wanted to mix things up to see how different methods worked. I just didn't have the time.

I chopped into the neck of one of them, then went in to the other. She heard me approaching and tried squiggling away. I knelt and put my hand on her shoulder, speaking so only she could hear. "You made the survivor's list. I'm going to give you the first treat." I began tugging the tape down to reveal the corner of her mouth and poured one of the little bottles of booze in. She gagged, not expecting the burn of alcohol, and I laughed at her. "The way you were pounding this stuff, I figured you'd be used to it."

I went through the others, working my finger between the adhesive and their skin to get enough room to empty the small containers before pressing the bindings back in place. When finished, I went back out to the car, reclined the front seat, and drifted off in my own dreamless sleep.

The sun woke me in the morning. It got a bit chilly overnight but had begun warming quickly. I stepped out and relieved myself, then went in to check on my party girls. Most had tried wiggling out of their bonds, the tape rolling together at the edges, but I had used a lot on each, so they couldn't get loose. Or so I thought.

One of them had gotten free, her room empty and the remains of tape on the floor. The strips I wrapped around her head had long blond hairs stuck to them and I knew it had to be the one I had not finished off the night before, the first I had given a drink to. Try to cut some people a break...

She didn't even try to get to me while I slept. I guessed she didn't want to chance waking me. I walked around to windows on different sides of the building, hoping to see her running away. Then, I discovered she tried to free two others before she made a break for it. Their makeshift fetters were bunched up in places, looking to be the parts where she attempted ripping the thick layers of tape.

"Good morning, ladies," I called out for all them to hear. "As some of you already know, one of your fellow traveling companions has slipped out of her room, and it looks as though she tried to free a couple of her friends." I began walking by each of them in turn, nudging with my boot the ones she tried to help. Both of them rewarded me with a whimper of acknowledgment. "I'm guessing she told you she was going to get help and she'd be back. I'm here to tell you, she won't make it.

"See, I chose this location for its remoteness; there is nothing around here but desert for miles on every side. So, I need to make sure nobody else can disappear while I retrieve her, but I'll be back. And I won't be bringing help."

I took out one of the daggers as I crept over to the nearest. Placing the tip on her chest between her massive tits, I slid it down toward her belly button, laying open her skin, but not pressing hard enough that her guts would spill out. The next, I rolled over and jammed the point directly into the lumbar region of her spine, hoping to paralyze her from the waist down.

One after the other, I caused some sort of damage to

ensure they wouldn't try to get free anymore. The pain would make the effort unbearable.

The Endgame

In Beth's dream, Mike had bound the women he had taken. The rooms were barren, the walls showed signs of long neglect and a thick layer of dust covered the dried-out wood of the floors.

Each of the captives had been trussed up with wide silver duct tape, hands bound behind their backs and feet tied together. More tape had been wrapped around their eyes and mouths, tight enough to bulge their cheeks out.

Mike went back to the bus and drove off, making his way back to the main road. He traveled for about ten minutes and she saw a long white building ahead. Two service bays, overhead doors rolled down to indicate they weren't taking jobs, occupied the nearest end, and a store/restaurant in the other. A group of three gas pumps rested half way between the ends.

Mike pulled in the near drive and went around back. He drove past a multitude of disabled and abandoned cars and trucks, headed to a line of buses looming on the other side. Pulling in between a couple of the bigger ones, he shut off the engine, grabbed a bag from beside him and left.

Beth saw him bend down several times to pick up some discarded, rusty tools and drop them into his bag, which already looked to contain a fair number of items from the way it sagged and swung, stretching the areas where the handle had been sewn on.

He went to the edge of the building behind the closed service bays and peeked around to the front. An old man stood at the pumps filling the tank of his long red four-door sedan. When he finished, he pulled to the far side and went in.

Mike double backed, making his way behind the store until he came to the line of windows for the eatery. He eased himself up from a crouched position and glanced in to see where the customers and staff were. Three men sat at the counter on uncomfortable looking stools, drinking coffee and flirting with the only waitress. A family occupied a booth closer to the door and the old guy had made his way to a smaller booth away from the noisy kids.

The waitress delivered plates laden with dinner items to the family, then went to get the newcomer's order. Mike ducked back down and slipped around the corner. Two cars occupied the spots closest to his end, probably the waitress and the cook, who could have also owned the place. Three pickup trucks parked next to each other and an old station wagon were next, then the town car at the far corner.

He made his way along the wall, keeping low, and veered to the driver's side of the sedan. Opening the door, he tossed his bag in and rummaged around for the keys before a glint from the floor caught his eye. The keys had been dropped beside the man's leg as he got out. Mike slid in, started the engine, slowly backed out and went back around and into the midst of the derelict piles of vehicles.

Beth watched as he went back into the tour bus and took one of the luggage bags, shook it empty and began putting water, beer, and small liquor bottles into it from the cooling fridge and shelves mounted in the rear. Then he got back in the car and left, using the same driveway he had entered.

She didn't know how accurate her dream would be but tried to pay attention to landmarks so she would know where the turns were. When he made it back to the big house, the sun neared the horizon. She saw him go in and check on the captives, then use a rusty hatchet he had picked up at the garage to chop the necks of two of them.

She sat bolt upright in her bed, Jason sitting beside her. She didn't recognize him in the dusky predawn light and began flailing at him, thinking he might be the killer dressed as Mike. He flinched and caught her hands, wrestling to get them down and calling her name to wake her up.

"What's the matter?" He asked. "Another dream?"

She glanced around as if to make sure they were alone in the room, then sat up and hugged him. She held back the tears as she told him of what she saw.

"I had a weird dream, too," he told her. "I guess it was the time frame before yours. I watched as he tied and taped them all down, then mutilate three of them before killing them." He turned from her and stood, pacing the small room. When he turned back to her, a sad look had overcome him. "I never told you, but I've seen the start of all his killings."

"What do you mean? All of them?"

He placed a hand on the back of his neck as he tilted his head back and to the sides. "Yeah," he whispered as he looked downward. "All of them."

She went to him and put her hand on his forearm. "Jason, we have to tell Bruce. If we can find Mike, maybe we can stop him before this goes any further."

He agreed and they got their stuff together. When they knocked on the door to wake Bruce, he flung it open before the third. "I heard some of what you talked about through the walls," he told them as he ushered them in. He leaned out and glanced both ways, then closed the door. Looking at Beth, he asked, "Do you really think you can find where he is?"

"I don't know. If we can get to the area, find where this store is that I saw, maybe."

Bruce took up his radio and called the others to get up and meet him at the cars in 30. They gathered outside, and just closed the trunk of the car Bruce drove, as Detective Maron pulled up in her brown Police SUV, the white doors stained with dirt buildup.

She came up, looking as if she had something on her mind. "Bruce, could I talk to you?"

"Actually, we were just heading to see if we could find a place to eat," he told her, swiping his arm around to indicate the whole group. "If you could recommend somewhere?" He left it open like an offer.

Maron caught on to his meaning. "Actually, I do know a place."

She led them to June's Diner, where she had been having her lunches for quite some time. The morning waitress looked a bit confused, almost afraid to open the doors for the group of huge men she had never seen before. Had Detective Maron not been there, Bruce felt sure she would have gotten a call from the middle-aged server.

As the lock disengaged, Maron told her, "Morning, Shell. I know you aren't open for a little while, but I needed a quiet place to talk to these people." Shell glanced at the dozen big men, then at the well-dressed young man and the beautiful girl next to him. They didn't look scared, at least not of their companions, so

Shell stood aside and led them to a back room.

There were several long tables set out, surrounded by six chairs each. "This is where we host special events. You can rearrange some to fit your needs if ya like. Does anyone need coffee?" She tried to keep her friendly smile and found it coming more naturally as all of them politely accepted.

When Shell went to get that going, they pulled three tables together and set chairs around. None of the other men knew about the dreams yet, so Bruce had Jason and Beth give a short history of the situation.

For an hour, the two shared what they knew, what had happened and how similar their dreams had ended up being to the events.

The cook had come out to check on them. Maron told him, "I know it's a bit early, Dave. Is there any way we could get a quick breakfast?"

The man looked at the hulking men sitting with her. "Looks like these guys could clean out an all-you-can-eat buffet line. If you could all do scrambled eggs, bacon, and toast, I could mass produce a big batch. Wouldn't take too long."

Bruce answered for his men, "That would be great. Thank you."

Dave went off to begin, and Shell came in to refill everyone's coffees. When she left, Maron turned back to topic.

"So, you're saying your dreams show what he's going to do?"

Jason responded, "So far, I've seen what he's done, I'm guessing either after he's done it or as it happens." The sorrow of witnessing the events showed in his eyes. "The actual results have verified, to me anyway, that what I dream is what happened. There are not many deviations.

"Beth, too, sees his actions, but since it is now her

boyfriend doing them, I think she's more attuned to his movements."

"Okay," Maron cut in, "here's where I'm sketchy." She held off while Dave and Shell brought in the food. A large tray of bacon, two platters of toast and three bins full of scrambled eggs. He asked if they needed anything else, and Bruce told him they would be fine, staving off any requests of the other men for additions. The two went back to preparing for the quickly approaching opening time.

Maron continued, "You say that the one who killed your sister, Beth, is not the one who did the truck stop?"

Beth nodded. "I know it's hard to believe. I wouldn't if I had not seen the change. Even then, I couldn't accept it until Jason gave me the back-story. It kind of makes sense, at least from where I sit." She had a challenging posture as she said it.

"My men," Bruce interjected, "have seen what this bastard did to Wriley. All but myself, Jones, and Quince. Neither Jason nor Beth saw Miss Canton, but both described the scenes found almost exactly."

Maron sat back after finishing her plate. She rubbed her chin with her thumb and forefinger as she thought. Leaning forward onto her elbows, she said, "Okay. Here's the deal. I'm going after him, but I need some backup. I can't very well take my entire department and leave no one here to handle business as usual, and I know better than going alone.

"I need to know, if I have your team help, that your men will follow directions."

"They will follow my directions, and if I tell them to follow yours, they will."

"We need to get going," Jason said. "Time is getting close to what I saw." He had dreamed that, an hour or so after sunrise, the killer had almost frantically gone through and slaughtered all the women, not following his usual MO of removing their breasts, but going from one to the other and using a hatchet to kill them.

They all stood and began filing out, each one thanking both the workers who served them. Jason brought up the rear and approached the register. Dave came up and said, "Susan is a regular here, there's no charge."

"Nonsense," he told them, taking out his wallet. He dropped five $100 bills saying, "You went through a lot of supplies, opened up early for us and," looking at Shell with a smile, "gave us great service. This is the least we can do." The two glanced from the cash to each other, and then to the young man's back as he went to join the others.

The group gathered at the police vehicle while Maron called in. Dispatch told her they had gotten a hit on the location of the bus and sent the directions to her cell. She then placed a call to the Sheriff to inform him she had enlisted help and was en route to the lo-jack position of the bus.

When she instructed the others to stay behind her, Bruce took the radio from William's rider and handed it to her.

"He took one of these when he got away from the Canton scene, but I think he might have turned it off. Either way, be careful what you broadcast."

They all sped off behind her, the blue and white strobes flashing but no siren. The GPS directions took them down the highway, then had them turn down a poorly paved road.

Beth perked up as she saw a landmark she recognized and pulled up the radio. "Detective, turn here."

"Are you sure? It's not the way the GPS says."

"I know this road. It's the one I saw him take in my dream."

Maron scoffed to herself, *Now, we're chasing a*

dream. Sounds like a song from the 80's. She did slow and make the corner, the others following suit. In the distance, a large, dilapidated house came into view. Maron called back, "Beth, are you sure about this?" She wanted to get to the location of the bus to try and figure out the next move. "The lo-jack positioning says the bus is ten miles farther."

"I'm telling you, this is the way to where they are."

The house loomed closer, not looking like it had been occupied for several decades. The line of sedans followed Maron as she turned in and parked in front. Bruce scanned the ground and saw the tire marks leading around the side of the building and called on the radio, "Tracks lead this way. Maron, keep Jess and Zack with you, check for survivors. William, you and Quince follow me."

"Check," Maron responded and motioned the men told to accompany her to enter the place.

Inside, she told them, "Be careful, we don't know for a fact the killer has left." She pointed teams to split off. "Groups of two, clear each room and check your fire. There could well be survivors."

The men nodded and split up, three teams on the first floor and the other three heading up the rickety stairs. She could hear below as the men cleared rooms as they reached the landing. She motioned the others to one end of the long hallway as she and her partner, Percy, took the other.

Each of the ones on the second level began calling they had a body, followed by the declaration that their find had died. Maron and Percy had the same results. The body count rose to ten with two rooms to go as the other group caught up with them.

"No survivors, Detective," the man called Kevin told her. The groups from below had come up to report they had found nothing down there, and they all entered the last room together. When they saw one of the victims hanging upside down, with her breasts sliced open and crumpled pouches on the floor beneath her, Kevin said, "What the hell are those?"

Maron walked over and touched one of the packets, and recoiled. "Silicone. Breast implants. He must have taken them out, but why did he empty," she didn't finish, as she looked at the wounds and saw the discolored fluid pooled in the depths. "Oh, shit. He emptied them back into her breast." She stood and backed away. Her foot hit an obstacle and a moan sounded. "We have a survivor here!"

Several of the men came to assist and she told them to stay with the lady so she could call for an ambulance.

Maron ran downstairs as fast as she dared and out to her cruiser. "Dispatch! Carol, are you there?"

"Go ahead," came the static filled reply.

"We found a survivor. Send an ambulance and tell the Sheriff we have three cars in pursuit of the perp."

After she got confirmation, she closed her door to return, but her boss came over the airwaves. "Maron, Whitaker here."

She picked up her mic, "Go ahead."

"I'm at the lo-jack position, we found the bus. Where are you?"

She didn't have time to go into particulars, so gave him the directions Beth had told her from her dream, describing the landmark indicating the turn. "When you see a rusted-out tractor on your right, turn left. You'll see the big house about two miles down."

"How the hell did you get there?" He almost sounded angry that she hadn't gone to the bus first.

"Long story, sir."

Bruce came over the two-way, "He's veered to the right. Quince, slow it down in case he heads back."

"Who is that?" Whitaker demanded.

"The group chasing the perp into the desert," she told him. "I thought it best I check the house for survivors so sent him and two other vehicles in his group to chase the perp." She heard gunfire in the distance.

"Quince, he gave us the slip," Bruce called. "Do you see him?" He got no response. "Quince! Jones, do you copy? The perp has gone back toward you. Jones! Answer me, damn it!"

She recognized William's voice, "Bruce, I see his cloud. He's cut to the north!"

Whitaker heard the exchange, as Maron had kept her mic open. "Maron, stay where you are. State units are with me. We're on the way. Carol, status on the EMS team?"

Carol confirmed they were headed to Maron's GPS location. Maron grabbed her handheld and called, "Bruce, Maron here. All the victims are dead but one. We have five mutilations matching the vic at the truck stop and seven others who've been executed without being disfigured."

"Roger, Maron." When he didn't elaborate, she headed back inside. Sirens in the distance told her the response teams were almost there.

A Survivor

The woman watched as the man who abducted them went from one of his captives to the other, slicing and stabbing to make them unable to struggle to get free as she had done.

This is all my fault, she thought. *If I hadn't escaped, he wouldn't be doing this.* She knew, though, that he intended to kill all of them anyway.

She should have run from the place, but when she got loose and went outside in the night, she could see nothing but desert for miles around by the partial moonlight.

She went back in, found a secluded spot, and cried herself to sleep. Thoughts of releasing others entered her weary mind, but they would have nowhere to go, either. He would catch them and do even worse things.

She woke to the sound of him declaring that she had gotten loose, and he needed to make sure none of them got free while he searched her out. She had to do something, she couldn't just cower and hope he didn't find her.

He took the gags off the others before mutilating them, listening to their screams of pain with perverse pleasure.

When he got to the last one, she decided to move. She grabbed a piece of board and crept up behind him as he knelt beside his final victim. He held a knife and plunged it into the woman's shoulder.

He saw the shadow sneaking up, arms raised holding a 2×4. When he saw the downward motion, he tucked and rolled to the side. The momentum of her swing could not be stopped, and the corner of the board drove into the temple of the trussed-up lady. Her skull caved in and blood gushed. The attacking woman dropped the wood, her hands going to her mouth in shock.

The killer lunged back at her and sliced through her side with the blade. She fell, clutching the wound and crying out as the man walked up beside her.

"Well, you made my work a little easier," he spoke softly. He reached down and grabbed a handful of her hair, lifting her into a crouch, then slid his fingers into her waistband and threw her toward the wall. The rotting clapboards gave with little resistance and her body went half-way through it. He walked to the other side and grabbed her blouse to pull her into the next room, the fabric tearing a little from the weight.

"So, you wanted to stop me?" His voice held a venomous tone that sent shivers through her injured body. He dragged her by the hair to the doorway of the room they had just left and pushed her down making her head bounce off the jam and stars flitter across her sight.

He went to get his bag and pulled out the broken sledge. He swung it to the area just above the door and made a hole, then did the same from the other side. Taking out more of the rope, he fed it through and tied it to the support, then tied a loop just under.

She watched as he went over to the nearest remaining

captive and grab her by the tape around her ankles, dragging her to the doorway and lifting her feet high enough to slide the rope under the tape. He fed the end through the loop and began hoisting her up. Her shoulders and head just cleared the ground and he tied another knot to hold her there.

When he bent close to the bruised and battered escapee, he said, "Now you get to watch." He grabbed a rusty, bloody saw from his bag and knelt beside the dangling woman.

He laid the saw down and went through the ceremony of unbuttoning her shirt and unhooking the clasp on her bra. Then, he grabbed her left breast and positioned the saw at the base.

"No," escaped the woman watching as she tried to reach and stop him, but he paused and leaned in toward the one tied up.

"Would you look at that?" Raising his voice above the whimpers and sobs of the others, he announced, "Ladies, it seems we have an impostor here. This one has had some surgery." He took a handful of her hair and lifted her slightly. "Let's see what you have in there, shall we?"

He dropped the saw and took out a rusty razor blade scraper. With utmost care, he sliced along the scar, taking one layer at a time until he got to the packet he wanted to find. He laughed louder than she screamed, "I knew it. You mean to tell me that you wanted to look like these other cows? You had shit stuffed into your tits to make them bigger?"

He repeated the process on her other breast. Bundling the pack in his hand, he pierced it and held open her wound. "Oh, my mistake. Here let me put it back." He began squeezing the silicone back into her, getting more pleasure from her heightened cries and jerking movements. Then did the same to her other tit.

Outside, he heard the revving of car engines slowing and accelerating, and he dashed to the window to look out. A line of vehicles had turned toward the house, led by a brown and white police SUV with several black sedans behind it. "How the hell?"

He went back to his hanging victim and called out, "It seems like I've run out of time. Now, you might be thinking I'm just going to leave and you'll all survive, but I have a different conclusion."

He swiped his blade across the throat of the hanger and kicked the runner in the jaw, causing it to jut to the other side with the crunch of the bone breaking. He pulled out the hatchet, took up his bag and went from one captive to another, slamming the dull, chipped blade on the necks of each one to drain them of their lives. When finished, he ran outside and jumped into the car.

Finale

Mike drove slow until he got around the building, then sped away into the barren wilderness. Pulling out the two-way, he turned it on to hear them calling to one another.

"Beth, are you sure about this?" The voice feminine with a gruff undertone. "The lo-jack positioning says the bus is ten miles farther."

A familiar voice came over, "I'm telling you, this is the way to where they are."

The killer looked in his mirror to see the cloud of dust grow larger at the front of the house. Then, "Tracks lead away this way," came from a deep voice he recognized as Bruce from Wriley's place. "Maron, keep Jess and Zack with you, check for survivors. William, you and Quince follow me."

"Check," came the gruff woman's voice, followed by two men affirming the directions.

Mike looked in his mirror again to see three cars coming around the house and taking up his tail. He pressed the pedal further, getting up as much speed as he dared without spinning out. His plume hid the chasers, but he knew they were there.

He veered to his right to find out how far behind him they were, then turned to the left and circled around to backtrack. The leader called over saying he saw the change of direction and told Quince to hang back.

The two cars sped past, not seeing their quarry passing going the other way. Mike pulled his pistol as the third car came into focus. As he passed, he took aim. The driver saw him too late and a bullet sprayed blood on the window as it entered his temple. The other side of his head exploded, spraying blood and brains over his companion.

Mike whipped his steering wheel to the left, then spun it far right, drifting the vehicle around to come along the passenger side of the stopped car. The second man stumbled out, coughing, and retching as he tried to yank his weapon from its holster. He brought it up too late, another shot caught him in his throat and splashed his neck bones with his blood over the top of their car.

Mike turned his wheel again and took off to the North.

"Quince, he gave us the slip. Do you see him?" Bruce yelled for his men to answer, calling for one then the other. "Jones! Answer me, damn it!"

"Bruce," said the one he remembered being called William, "I see his cloud. He's cut to the north!"

The killer saw the leading vehicles slow as they dwindled in the reflection, then turned in his direction to follow again. He kept glancing back, using his mirror and turning to look over his shoulder.

The female came across the waves again, "Bruce, Maron here. All the victims are dead but one. We have five mutilations matching the victim at the truck stop and seven executed."

"Roger, Maron."

Gahdammit, the fugitive thought, *why couldn't that bitch die like the rest?*

Bruce, with Jason and Beth in his car, stepped on the accelerator pedal, pushing it to the floor. William followed suit as his boss pulled forward.

They were gaining on the other car when they saw it drop out of sight. As they neared, Bruce called on the radio, "William, stop!" They both skidded to a halt just before going over the same ledge that caught Mike off guard.

They all piled out and looked over. The red town car lay at the bottom of a ravine, upside down. Steam rose from the busted radiator. "Look," said William, pointing down. They saw a figure crawling out of the wreckage.

Bruce went to the trunk of his car and pulled out a rifle. He took the covers off the scope and returned to the ledge. Taking aim, he pulled the trigger firing three rounds and missing. A shot rang out from below, and William's companion fell, his cheek pierced and the back of his head missing.

"Son of a bitch," William cried as he ducked for cover from the next shot. Another blast sounded, Beth's shoulder split open and Bruce caught her before she hit the ground.

He thrust the rifle into Jason's hands and pointed downhill. "Kill that fucking asshole before he takes the rest of us down!" He tore open his shirt and ripped a section off his tee to press against her wound.

Jason edged closer and took aim. He fired two more shots and missed. Bruce took out the small replacement magazine and tossed it to him. "Six more shots. Take him out, damn it!"

He pulled the empty mag out and slapped the next one in. As he sighted through the scope, he got a better idea. Repositioning, he rapid-fired four rounds into the exposed gas tank.

"Ha!" The deep voice came from below. "Jason, a marksman you are not."

"We'll see," Jason mumbled and zeroed in on the expanding puddle of gas.

He remembered from his teens when he and his buddies would go into the foothills of the mountain surrounding the casino, shooting his .22 at the cliffs to hit some of the exposed flint rocks. The resulting shower of sparks got them all cheering, and they took turns trying to get the biggest display. The flashes were even more brilliant as the skies darkened with dusk. That had been with a little bullet, and he held a .30-.30 in his hands this time.

He looked through the scope and found the hard, shiny surface he knew all too well. Waiting for more liquid to pool around it, he heard the whiz of another shot from below and flinched, the shot he had begun to squeeze going wide. The man below hollered in pain. The errant round had caught him instead.

Jason took sight at the stone again and pulled the trigger. A bright spark flared and caught the fuel around it, expanding quickly and flowing into the trunk. A hollow whoosh sounded as the gas remaining in the tank lit, then it exploded. The entire car bounced off the ground with the force, and everything within a ten-foot radius caught fire; weeds, sand, killer, and all.

A mushroom cloud of smoke and flame billowed up. The people above recoiled as a large face formed in front of them, a smoky hand reaching toward Jason trying to latch on and take him over. The heat from the fire took it up too fast and the fingers clutched with no hope of catching any of them. They all watched as the blackness within kept rising until it dissipated in the upper atmosphere.

Jason turned to Bruce, who had Beth's head in his lap as he kept some pressure on her wounded shoulder. "I think I got him," he said with a grin.

"Cocky asshole." Bruce tried to look serious but his smile of approval gave him away. "We need to get Beth some medical care."

He picked her up as Jason returned the rifle to the trunk. Bruce told William to head back to the mansion to let the others know they had completed the mission. He laid the girl in the back seat and Jason slid in to hold the makeshift bandage to her while Bruce got behind the wheel.

They drove back to the mansion, arriving just as more police cars pulled up, followed by two ambulances and the coroner van. They let one pair of emergency technicians take over the care of Beth and walked inside to check with the other group.

Detective Maron stood talking with the Sheriff, filling him in on the particulars. When she saw the two men come in, she waved them over. "Sheriff Whitaker, this is Jason Makeland and Bruce Bellhouse. They are the leaders of the group who stuck to the killer's trail."

The men shook hands. Sheriff Whitaker asked, "Is it done then?" Bruce nodded and told them of the result, not sure how they would take the news of the image in the cloud, but not leaving it unsaid. "Hmph," replied the Sheriff. "We're going to need a formal statement from all of your men. Will they corroborate all this?"

"They will tell what they each know. Nothing more, nothing less. I'll authorize them to give you full disclosure." Bruce went to gather his men and issue the directions.

Maron had gone to check on Beth. Whitaker looked at Jason, "That's quite a story, young man."

"Oh, Sheriff," Jason replied, "you don't even know the half of it."

<<<<<The End>>>>>

About Your Author

John T. M. Herres was born May 26, 1965, to a military family.

His father served in the Air Force, and the family moved around a great deal during John's younger years – which meant a constant change of circumstances.

John tries to use these experiences to add richness and realism to his writing.

Influenced by such authors as Robert E. Howard, Stephen King, Dean R. Koontz, and James Patterson, his genre of choice became action/fantasy-adventure populated by barbarians inspired by Conan, et al, set in rich, exotic landscapes, though he dabbles in other genres.

John's writing has emerged and matured into works with three-dimensional characters, action sequences that read like a movie scene with great visuals for the reader, and plot lines that pull the reader deep into both the action and the psyche of his heroes.

John has written several poems and is dabbling with a sci-fi story, as well as some short stories in the horror genre.

Having lived in the Great state of Texas a majority of his life, he currently resides in Mississippi. His works-in-progress include "Tales of The Barbarian" and "Challenge of The Velah" which he is hoping to have published at some point.

Recently, a few of his writings have been accepted for publication by J Ellington Ashton and HellBound Books.

He also has self-published a poetry book through Xlibris (warning), available on Amazon and other online retailers. On his Amazon Author page one will find links to several Anthologies that include some of his short stories.

Other HellBound Books Titles
Available at: www.hellboundbookspublishing.com

Blood in The Woods

Based upon true events...

For Jody, growing up in the late eighties and early nineties in the small Louisiana town of Hammond with his best friend Jack was filled with wonderful childhood memories.

Time spent playing in the woods, shooting pellet guns, blowing up mailboxes, fighting at school and upon the dawning of interest in the fairer sex, their carefree lives typical of children with few responsibilities and no worries beyond the next pop-quiz or getting to second base. As they grow older together and experience the joys and pains of life, love, family and friendship, they uncover a grim secret that their home town has kept, and through little more than an innocent, idle curiosity, Jody and Jack stumble upon something horrific in the woods and their lives quickly take a most sinister and dangerous turn as they find themselves hunted by an unspeakable evil...

Them

Ray Sanders returns home from Florida to bury his mother.

Soon, the supernatural evidence behind his mother's demise begins to surface in the form of dreams and mysterious happenings.

During all of the madness, Sanders must face his destiny and vanquish the generations-old evil that has plagued his family since the 1800's…

In 1854, Louis Sanders, with the help of Elias Atkins, dug a well to provide water to the family farm. What they did not anticipate was the water to be infested with Odomulites - ancient sins. These malevolent beings - were trapped in our world on their way to the spirit world - formed a pact of protection with both Sanders and Atkins; the families would serve as guardians of the Odomulite nests and in return, a blind eye would be cast when the Odomulites took host bodies to inhabit and feed upon. It was this pact, which in 2016 would propel Sanders and Julie Fontaine - a young woman with a special connection to the Spirit World - into the heart of the last active nest to rid the town of its insidious Odomulite population.

Southern House

"Move over Slender-man, there's a whole new reason to be afraid of the dark!"

There are some places that lie where the barrier between worlds is thin and growing thinner. These corridors are as old as the Earth itself, hidden in dark and forgotten places, waiting to be found. There is a being who stalks these places and travels between those worlds. He was given the name Mr. Shift by generations of children and madmen. Just as Hickory Grimble hits rock bottom, he inherits his grandparents' farm and believes his luck is changing. He soon finds he inherited more than money and land. Haunted by his own inner demons, now he has new problems. He begins to see strange creatures on the dark, sprawling acreage, animals that have no business living in middle Tennessee. He also discovers a decrepit, abandoned house in the forest that never seems to be in the same place twice. Balanced on a razor's edge be-tween, addiction and fate, Hick is now face to face with an ancient evil that has returned once more to claim more of the town's children.

Worship Me

Something is listening to the prayers of St. Paul's United Church, but it's not the god they asked for; it's something much, much older.

A quiet Sunday service turns into a living hell when this ancient entity descends upon the house of worship and claims the congregation for its own.

The terrified churchgoers must now prove their loyalty to their new god by giving it one of their children or in two days time it will return and destroy them all.

As fear rips the congregation apart, it becomes clear that if they're to survive this untold horror, the faithful must become the faithless and enter into a battle against God itself.

But as time runs out, they discover that true monsters come not from heaven or hell…
…they come from within.

These Walls Don't Talk, They Scream

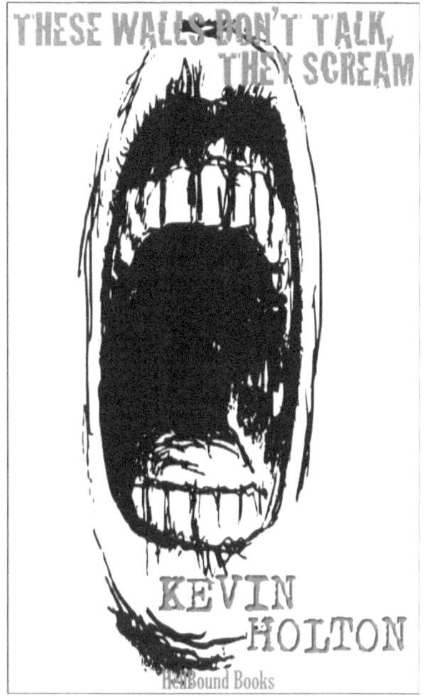

When three-year-old Charlotte witnessed her mother's death and was left alone with the body, she began hearing the voice of a person living in the walls of her house.

This voice comforted her as best it could, guiding her to call 9-1-1. Twenty five years later, Charlotte has returned with her own family to reconnect with this presence.

The recent death of her son leaves her distracted and mourning, though, so she doesn't realize her daughter can hear this entity too.

The Children of Hydesville

When the malevolent entity that Maggie and Katie Fox unleashed in Hydesville in 1848 returns in 2018, it must be stopped - at all costs.

Manhattanites Derek David and his wife Edith receive an invitation to visit the Keilgarden Colony, a secluded community located five hours north of the city in the village of Hydesville.

Dedicated to nurturing children with psychic abilities, the colony was built in 1948 on land that includes the cottage where Maggie and Katie Fox first heard the ghostly rappings in 1848 - which started the Spiritualist movement.

But what begins as a late-summer respite swiftly turns into a confusing and terrifying ordeal as Derek and Edith experience increasingly bizarre and disturbing events, which drives Derek to set fire to the Fox house.

Months later, New York Times reporter Sheila Irving and her boyfriend, Kevin Jackson, visit Hydesville to investigate Derek's motivation. If those gathered in the village succumb to the powerful entity that controls the area, they will partake in the creation of union children - psychically gifted offspring whose malevolent powers will reach far beyond the confines of the small township.

Schlock! Horror!

An anthology of short stories based upon/inspired by and in loving homage to all of those great gorefest movies and books of the 1980's - that golden age when horror well and truly came kicking, screaming and spraying blood, gore & body parts out from the shadows...

It was the decade that brought us everything in the cinema and on VHS from the Italian 'nasties' to *Elm Street, The Lost Boys, Hellraiser, The Thing, Day of the Dead, Reanimator, Return of the Living Dead, My Bloody Valentine, Henry: Portrait of a Serial Killer, Cannibal Holocaust*….and superlative directors such as David Cronenburg, John Waters, Roger Corman and - of course - Clive Barker.

All of this was, naturally, reflected in the books we devoured - Guy N Smith, Clive Barker's *Books of Blood*, James Herbert, Jack Ketchum, Gary Brandner and Richard Laymon, to name but a mere handful.

This 80's themed/inspired tales of terror is compiled by one Mr. **Bret McCormick**, himself a writer, producer and director of many a schlock classic, including *Bio-Tech Warrior, Time Tracers, The Abomination, Ozone: The Attack of the Redneck Mutants* and the inimitable *Repligator*.

A HellBound Books LLC Publication

http://www.hellboundbookspublishing.com

Printed in the United States of America